SLIDING IN

SEAN MORIARTY

The smell of dirt, grass and leather. It's unmistakable, there is no other smell like this one.

The smell of beer, hotdogs, popcorn, peanuts and soda... They surround me like an aura.

Only one other smell excites me as much as this and that's the one between a woman's thighs.

The screaming fans, the angry stares and the loud booing almost give me a hard-on.

Fuck, playing baseball is better than any drug I've ever heard of.

My game is on fire tonight; I can hear the fans feeling it too. My body is fucking sexy, it's all muscle and tendons. Working to create fucking perfection. My throwing arm is a work of art. It's what gives me the ability to stand here, under the lights, playing baseball.

Right here is where I love to be.

It's the top of the eighth inning.

Normally I don't go this long on the mound, but I'm

working on a no hitter right now and I feel pretty fucking good about it.

No one is on base so I get to stare down the batter for a moment, then I look to the catcher.

He is signing me to throw a fast ball high and to the right. Same fucking throw as the last time I pitched to this guy—Suarez—fucker hit it pretty damn well. Thankfully, the ball went far right into foul territory.

So why throw the same damn pitch? I keep wondering to myself.

Shit. I hate fucking throwing to Raleigh. We have two catchers on the team and this jackass doesn't give a shit about what I want. He should have been traded off the fucking team long before now, especially with how damn well we've been doing this season.

We were going to trade him... then didn't. From what I heard, it was either him or two prospects we have in the minors, and the Cleveland Hawks wanted the prospects.

They know Raleigh is an over-priced turd.

I shake my head to tell him *no*. There is no reason to throw that pitch right now, that's just asking trouble.

My fastball is fucking beautiful, but not if I've been pitching for eight innings and the fucker has the timing down on my throw.

He signals the same pitch twice more before he gives me the sign for a slider to the left and away.

How the fuck can he not understand that we need to throw something different?

I stand up, and just as I'm reaching back I see Raleigh move his mouth. I have no clue what the fuck he says but just as I'm throwing the ball, Suarez gives me a big smile.

It's too late to change what I am throwing.

And after I throw, Suarez connects with the ball.

Shit.

I turn towards the third base line and I'm helpless as I watch Hernandez dive to catch the ball.

Thank the fucking gods of baseball diamonds he is talented. He catches a fast hopping ball and spins to throw to first.

I turn with the ball, watching it reach the first baseman, Rich Smart, and he catches it.

It's a split second too late though.

The first base umpire swing his arms out to the side. "Safe!"

God dammit!

Looking over at the guy standing on first fucking base, I let out a growl. That shithead should not be fucking standing there. He's standing there, grinning to the base coach about how he got a base on me.

Fucker just ended the no-hitter I had going.

I held the Robins until the eighth but they still got one on me. Next time I throw against Suarez, I might just throw at him instead. Leave a bruise on that big fucking shoulder of his.

That's if I don't put a fucking hole through Raleigh first.

Turning away from the guy standing on first, I look to my dugout and see the manager Jim Harrison twirling his finger in the air.

"Fuck!" I growl out loud.

So that's it for me tonight? That's how this game is going to fucking end?

A win for the team but missing out on my no-hitter because Raleigh is a jackass.

Jim jogs up the stairs from the dugout. Raleigh has a snide grin on his face as he slowly saunters up to the mound I am standing on.

I would love to punch his smirking fucking mouth right now, maybe knock out a couple of teeth.

"Don't fucking ignore the signs I call, Crass," he says.

"Did you fucking tip him off?" I growl at him.

He doesn't bother to answer as Jim Harrison comes up to us.

"That was some great throwing..." Jim starts to say, but I quickly talk over him.

"I asked if you fucking tipped him off, Raleigh," I say very loudly this time as I roll my shoulder.

Fucker could have hurt my damn arm pulling shit like that.

There is a small twinge from where I tried to adjust the pitch. Adjusting it didn't work and now it feels like I may have strained it.

Jim looks shocked for a moment as the words register with him. We may be in a stadium full of loud rabid fans but he fucking heard me. I don't doubt some of the guys heading to the pitcher's mound heard it too.

Raleigh, for his part, does try to act innocent, but he doesn't do it well.

Raising his hands, he says, "All I know is I called for a slider to the right, you through too wide. Suarez hit it."

"That's fucking bullshit and you know it!" I say as I step towards him.

Jim and Felicio Hernandez are quick to get between us and Jim pushes me back towards the dugout.

Raleigh is all smirks until he hears Jim say very

loudly, "Don't worry, Crass, if he pulled shit like that it will show up on the video."

Mother fuck. I had a damn no-hitter going.

Rolling my shoulder again, I still feel something, but I don't think it's too bad. Least it doesn't feel injured, just strained. Like I over did it.

I don't bother with the bench as I head past the guys in the dugout. They all have questioning looks in their eyes but don't ask as I head further down the stairs towards the long hallway to the locker room.

An athletic trainer is rubbing my shoulder and checking everything over as I lay down on one of their tables.

From here, I'm able watch the rest of the game.

We win like I knew we would. Shit, it would be kind of hard to blow the lead we had going into the bottom of the eighth—six to nothing. Not a bad score for the evening, not a bad score at all. But it's hard not to be bitter about missing out on my no-hitter.

I watch as the guys filter in, I'm waiting for one guy in particular. I almost think he skipped out completely before I see him coming through the door.

Pushing the trainer away from me, I stand up from the table and head over to Jeff Raleigh. "What the fuck were you thinking tipping him off?"

There are guys instantly between us, and it's pretty damn clear Raleigh doesn't like the attention he's getting. He isn't smirking now.

"Fuck off, Crass. I didn't do shit."

I look around me at the guys standing between us,

and I really do want to push through them to strangle that fucker.

"You ever pull shit like that again, I will beat you senseless, you stupid fuck," I say, barely keeping it below a yell.

"I didn't do shit. You just lost your edge against him."

"I lost my what?"

"That's right, you fu—" Raleigh starts but doesn't get to finish.

"That's enough, gentlemen!" Our manager, Jim, yells to us.

Pointing to me, Jim says, "Shower now. Go home."

He points over to Raleigh. "I'm going to watch the game film. Anything fishy happens with that pitch and I'm going to see it."

"Whatever," Raleigh says as he turns from us and heads to his locker.

Nodding my head to Jim, I say "I wouldn't feel this twitch shit in my shoulder if I hadn't tried to throw it to a different spot. He tipped Suarez."

Turning away from the whole fucking mess, I rub my temples. My head hurts and I really want to get the fuck out of here right now.

Walking past Emilio Hernandez, I ask "You want to go get a couple of beers?"

"Hell yeah," he smiles to me.

He's my party buddy most nights.

The team pretty much insists if we go out drinking we have another guy with us for safety reasons and to keep our shit out of the press.

We get a couple more of the guys who aren't married

pussies to go and it looks like it will be a fun night. We are all single and ready to fuck after our win.

———

We hit three different clubs tonight, and each club got disgustingly worse.

Not a single fresh face for me to stick my dick into.

Fuck.

After a night like tonight, I really need to release some inner pressure and blow a wad out of my balls.

Fuck, I would even suffer through just a blow job if I could get some kind of pressure release right now.

Nothing is going my way today.

Emilio is doing fucking amazing though. He's latched onto some sexy little blonde piece of ass, and I am pretty sure he is going to try knocking her ass up from the way they are moving on the dance floor. Fuck, I am surprised they are still clothed.

The end of the night comes to a close. My head is starting to hurt and all the beer I've drank is souring in my stomach.

I nod to Hernandez as he heads to his black Porsche with the little blonde. "See ya Thursday."

We are off tomorrow and I don't pitch again until Thursday. I could go in and work out but I just don't fucking feel like it right now. This whole thing with Raleigh has me mad as fire. Jim should be able to see what I was talking about.

I climb in my Lexus and I try to not puke out the liquid swirling around in my stomach. I'm far from drunk though, I don't even have a buzz.

"Fuck," I mutter. I need to eat something to soak up all this cheap swill I've drank or I am going to be sick in the morning.

I push the car into gear and ease out of the parking lot. This is one of those clubs, though, that isn't in the nicest parts of town, so I don't feel like a pussy when I lock the doors.

We rarely come here, it's usually our last-ditch effort to find some pussy or get too drunk to care. I didn't do either so now I get to be the lone guy.

Everyone else either found someone or went home after the second club. Even if we are off tomorrow we still need to rest.

I'm not too far away from the club or the seedier part of town when I spot an all-night diner sign lighting up the night like a beacon from the gods. Food. Food will be good for me.

Looking around my car, I make sure I won't be mugged the moment I get out. I'm too damn good looking to be mugged by some asshole.

Walking through the glass doors, the restaurant is mostly empty. I see two older guys sitting next to each other at the long counter, and a small older lady at the register dozing.

Sitting myself down at one of the booths, I lean my head back and blow out a long sigh of air.

Fuck the game.

Fuck tonight.

And fuck just about everything.

I smell more than hear my waitress come up to the booth. I'm pretty sure she thinks I am asleep by all the muttering she does.

She smells so fucking good though. All around me are the smells of a greasy spoon type of diner, but she smells like flowers and all woman.

Sitting up, I take in what has to be one of the most beautiful women I have ever seen in my entire life. Fucking hell, I've never seen a woman this damn hot.

Fuck me. I want to fuck her.

She looks tired as shit and maybe a bit annoyed with me already because I'm just staring at her... but wow. She's on the shorter side of things, pale skinned, red haired, blue eyed and lightly freckled fucking perfection. She is hot. Hot like I want to put my babies in her hot so I can keep her for myself.

"What can I get for you?" she asks, and for the first time in a very long time I don't have any words.

Well I do, but they are all filthy and about what I want to do with her body on top of the table right now.

"Your name, number and when you get off for starters?" I give her my best smile.

Heh, I'm pretty sure I know when she will get off.

Right after my face gets between those thighs of hers.

What a bad night.

It's slow and the only customers that have showed up are the two guys sitting at the counter - Joe and Bob, my regulars.

More like *regularly don't tip,* to be honest. Why they come here to eat, bitch to each other and not bother to tip is beyond me. I make it a point to tip when I am out eating away from home. I know just how much a tip means to a waitress.

Ugh, to crap with it. Tonight is going to be yet another wash, I can just feel it. We don't even get a crowd from the night clubs.

This just sucks.

I really need to talk to Tony about switching to first or second shift.

At first, I did this stupid third shift as a way to go to classes for college and to be home for grandma during the day. Those two things are still needed but grandma has improved to the point now where I could work in the mornings and take some night classes.

The only thing keeping me on this shift is the stupid hope it would provide money like it does during the school year.

It doesn't.

I set the steak with fries in front of Joe, then the burger with fries in front of Bob. Same thing they get every night they come in.

I really want to pull the plates out from under their faces as they dig in, then tell 'em to tip me if they want to eat...

But I don't.

Inside my head I am so much bitchier and mean than I could ever be in real life. Well, perverted too, but that's an entirely different issue all together.

In my head, I snatch those plates away and give 'em a good smirk. Instead, I turn around, fake smile in place, and grab the coffee pot to refill their quickly emptying cups.

They both give me the stink-eye as if I'm interrupting them or something.

Big stupid jerks.

Damn, when Tony comes in this morning, I am asking him to switch my shifts as soon as he can.

I clean all the table tops and the empty space at the counters one more time before I have nothing left to do.

I did all the busy work earlier. Silverware rolled, salt shakers filled. Plates stacked. Thankfully, the bathrooms were cleaned on the shift before mine.

I have nothing left to do but stand here and look out the window.

Time crawls by.

In a matter of minutes, Joe and Bob have scraped their plates clean, and now they are back to sipping their coffee and bitching about the current state of the world.

I head over to grab their empty plates and carry them into the kitchen.

By the time I've put the dishes up and come back, I see a customer has walked by Doris and seated himself at one of the tables.

Holy shit, he is good looking too. Damn. I was completely prepared for a night of grumpiness, and now there is a sexy guy waiting in one of my booths for me.

Maybe this night is looking up?

As I walk over though, I notice his head is tipped back and his eyes are closed. He looks either drunk or asleep with his big body sprawled out in the booth like he owns the place.

And... my enthusiasm instantly dampens.

Okay, drunk is not sexy, not sexy at all.

My mom and dad were high functioning alcoholics, and they died because of it. I've made a vow to myself to never fall for an alcoholic, no matter how hot he is. Not ever. It's just not worth it.

Walking up to him, I stand there for a moment and stare at the bulging muscles of his forearms. They're crossed over his large... well, okay... massive chest. This guy is in peak, physical shape. A prime example of the best the male sex has to offer women.

He's all muscles and smooth, lickable skin. Even his face is nice to look at. A smooth brow and straight nose. There's a thick, dark beard covering most of his chin but it's trimmed and well-kept.

Why does he have to be so hot *and* a drunk? I really don't like how my body is responding to him.

His eyes open and lock on me. They're gorgeous baby blues.

Shit.

"What can I get for you?" I ask hurriedly.

I'm anxious to take his order so I can get away from him. I need some space between us.

The longer I'm standing here, the more and more I feel like I'm being sucked into his orbit.

The menu is splayed on the table in front of him but he doesn't even glance at it.

Instead, Mr. Sexy opens his mouth and says, "Your name, number and when you get off for starters?"

He can't be serious?

I want to be polite to this jack ass, in fact my job pretty much depends upon it but I've had it.

For the first time in a long time my mouth opens up and I have no control of what comes out of it.

"Really? That's the absolute best you could do?" I roll my eyes, showing I'm totally not impressed. "*Smooth.* Where'd you learn that one? Dating 101 for jackasses?"

I don't know what came over me and immediately feel a little embarrassed I responded that. I should be used to this kind of stuff from all the students who come in here late at night after hitting the clubs during the school year.

But right now, I'm just not in the mood to deal with it, especially from him.

What's worse is that I'd probably be tempted if he had said something a little more clever.

He grins widely, not even the least bit fazed by my

attitude. Glancing down at the menu, he says, "Two steaks, medium. Fries and a... is your tea fresh?"

The fact that's he's not bothered by my attitude even a smidgen bothers me enough that I don't tamp it down when I open my mouth.

Fuck, why does he just have to be all cool and just roll with it? Why couldn't he have said something else stupid?

"No, it's bitter and stale," I snark.

Okay, now I'm really sounding like a bitch. I should seriously try to tone it down a bit. But fuck, the way he's looking at me and grinning is getting all my motors going.... And lubricated.

If he didn't literally smell like he just walked out of a brewery, I might be able to let myself forget that he's a drunk.

He smiles again at me and winks. "Sounds good..." Leaning in he reads my name tag, "Clarissa."

Our eyes meet and hold. It's like there's this strong current of electricity flowing between us and I'm rooted to the spot.

As his lips begin to curve in a cocky smirk, I realize I'm just standing here like some love-struck fool and clear my throat. "Anything else?"

"Is your pie any good?" he asks. He doesn't exactly leer at me, but he does stare deeper into my eyes. Shit. He is way too hot to be such a pervert.

Thighs clenching, I grit out, "Our apple is the best, the rest are okay."

"I'll have two slices of that too for dessert," he says then refolds his arms across his chest.

Those muscles of his are oh-so thick and too damn sexy.

"Okay, I'll..." I stammer out for a moment and then mentally bitch slap my face. "I'll be right back with your drink."

Turning away from him, I can feel his eyes watching my ass as I walk away. Damn. I feel almost naked to him right now.

Your name, number and when you get off for starters... I snort to myself, trying to get a grip. Was that for real?

I return with his tea and quickly walk away, avoiding any further conversation with him but even after being around him for only a moment, I feel like I just flew too close to the sun.

Heading into the kitchen, I pick up a rag and start wiping down the counters just to have something to do. I can see the whole diner from back here but the corner blocks out his table. Which is good. I don't need his eyes following me around the entire time I'm trying to work.

Just taking his drink to the table I felt like he was using them to mentally eat me up.

His food is ready too quickly for my tastes but he is the only one Miguel, the cook, is making food for right now.

Taking the plates with me, I slowly walk to his table and bend over, setting them down in front of him.

Part of me wants to ask where he's going to put all that food but I don't bother. With the way he is built I have no doubt he will just work it off.

"Thanks, Clarissa," he says, and I just nod before I spin around. Then his deep, cocky voice stops me as he adds, "You still haven't told me what time your shift ends."

Slowly, I spin back around and try to give him my best

I'm so not interested look. "It ends sometime in the morning."

He grins. "What do you feel like doing after I pick you up?"

"I'd rather throw myself off a bridge."

Shit, I know my cheeks are red as I realize that just came out of my mouth. It was supposed to stay in my head, dammit.

He only smiles all the more. "Nah, that would hinder us getting to know each other."

I shake my head and walk away from him. I try my best to make sure my ass doesn't sway behind me but if I try too hard I will look like a duck.

Damn, I do not like this man. My bitchiness isn't working on him; he doesn't seem the least bit repulsed. If anything, I think it might be turning him on!

I fill the guys at the counter up with coffee and then I retreat safely back into the kitchen with Miguel.

Miguel is a big man, and very quiet. His wife though is a real talker. Miguel once told me he likes nights because it gets him time away from all the talking. I like that about Miguel. When it's just us and Doris we all fall into a steady but comfortable quiet.

I march out a bit later with Mr. Sexy's apple pie slices, a fresh glass of tea and his check.

"Anything else I can get for you?" I ask as almost an afterthought.

"Are you hiding in the back because of me?" he asks and for the first time I realize how deep and gravelly his voice is.

Sexy looks, sexy voice and such a waste of space in that big sexy head.

"No." I lie right to him.

"Fibber."

"Wha...Did you jus...Fibber? Are we nine?" I sputter. Seriously, I've got nothing else.

He stands up from the table. Glancing down at his watch he frowns for a moment.

Holy shit he is tall. I am five foot five and he's at least six-two.

Looking up to him this close causes my neck to twinge, and my stomach feels all fluttery and nervous. He's just straight up huge...

He pulls his wallet from his back pocket and extracts a single green bill from it.

From the corner of my eye I catch the bill dropping to the table. For some odd reason I just can't take my eyes off his face.

Like an idiot, I just stand there, gaping up at him. I don't know why but there's this intense feeling of expectation and longing in my chest.

Once again, I've allowed myself to get sucked into his orbit, and now that I'm there all I really want to do is stay there.

He bends forward a little and I hold my breath.

I don't like him, I remind myself. He's too cocky, too sexy, too arrogant.

But I have the strongest urge to lift up on my tiptoes, meet him halfway and kiss him.

His baby blue eyes flash as if he can see exactly what I'm thinking through my eyes. His lips begin to curve and I'm suddenly fascinated by them. They look so soft, so pillowy, I bet it would feel really good to kiss them.

Then he straightens to his full height, pulling away.

The connection between us breaks, and damn if I don't feel disappointed.

"Have a good night, Clarissa. I'll see you again soon," he says in that deep, gravelly voice of his like it's a promise.

I bite my tongue to keep myself from saying something else snarky. He's almost gone, I don't need to be giving him any more reasons to linger.

And I sure as hell don't need to be asking him why he didn't just kiss me like I wanted.

I watch him walk away, his ass looking amazing in the designer jeans he's wearing.

Really, I wish I could find just one thing about him that isn't sexy besides his drinking. Would it be too much for the gods to give him a flat ass or a bald spot?

I even watch him as he hops into his expensive little sports car, not turning away until our eyes meet through the windshield and he winks at me.

I hear his engine revving up, then he's pulling away. Now that he's out of my life, I can finally breathe.

Glancing down at the table, I pause. There's a hundred-dollar bill just lying there.

A hundred dollars... That asshole.

I hated to get out of there so quickly, but after glancing down at my watch I saw I had a text from Jim Harrison from much earlier in the night. I must have missed it during the club crawl. The text told me to be at the club house at eight a.m.

Fuck. That's... I look at the watch on the car's dashboard and frown. It's three now.

Shit.

Getting home takes a bit because of how far I live away from the stadium. I am one of the few guys who live outside of the city. I don't like being close to neighbors so I live in the hills instead. One of the major pluses is the fantastic view I get of the city. It allows me to look out on the city, but not have to live down in the cluster of people.

Pulling in through the privacy fence, I pull my car into the double garage. Parking beside my black custom built motorcycle—it's loud and abrasive just like me.

Crawling into bed is pretty easy after the shower. I can't go in smelling like booze and cigarettes.

Sliding into my sheets, I frown.

I wish that little red headed minx was in bed with me right now. She would fit perfectly straddled across my hips, riding my thick dick.

My cock is semi-hard and grumping at me as I fall asleep.

Not much more than three hours later I'm awake with the shrill sound of my phone's alarm going off. This is going to be a long day.

Fuck, a real long day.

I'm off from pitching, but I still need to work out and hunt down Clarissa. Just the thought of her name has my morning dick waking up. Stirring with memories of faint dreams involving her naked body. Whatever I was dreaming must have been good because my body is tensed up, ready to be set loose on her.

Showering and stroking one out is a tempting thought but this tension isn't enough to force my hand into taking drastic measures just yet.

I honestly can't remember the last time I jerked off.

Shit, I never have to.

Damn, I think as I gaze down at the hard bastard.

I should have tried to get her to come home with me.

The parking lot under near the stadium for employees and players is close to the front office. I've been in here multiple times, but this time feels different. I haven't been called down to the office before like I was last night... So whatever is going on must be pretty serious.

What Raleigh did last night was way beyond fucked up.

I pull my gym bag out of the backseat and head into the building. There are a couple of cars around but not a lot. Most of the guys will be here soon to exercise and get ready for the day.

I keep my spirits up though; I didn't fuck up. I didn't even take a swing at the pile of shit. I walk through the front doors and the little cute receptionist points me back to Jim's office.

Straight to the man it is then.

Giving two quick knocks on the door frame, I stick my head in to see Jim and Art Manning inside talking together. Jim is our manager, and Art Manning is the GM and owner of the team—Jim's boss.

Well, shit on me.

They both turn to me as I step in.

Art speaks first as he walks over to me. He is a tall man, but I'm still a bit taller. He looks at me while shaking my hand. "How's the arm feeling today, Jackson?"

"Pretty good, sir."

"That's grand. Have a seat. We want to have a quick talk with you." He motions to a chair in front of the desk and I quickly head over there.

No sense in fucking about if the head guy is here.

"Good seeing ya, Jackson," Jim says as he sits down across from me.

Art takes the chair beside me and motions me to turn to the side a bit so we can be in a triangle to talk. Well, shit. This is going to be odd.

Nodding my head, I say to Jim, "You too, sir."

"Jackson, we wanted you down here today to talk about last night. That was a very serious accusation you made last night about Mr. Raleigh," Art starts off.

"Something was..." I start to defend myself but Jim makes a quiet cough and I quickly shut up.

It's going to be one of those *keep silent* kind of talks, I take it.

Art continues, "It is quite upsetting to think a team-mate would be willing give information to an opposing team. We have watched those tapes a few times, Jim and myself. We spoke with the Umpire, and tried speaking with Suarez, but as you can imagine he wasn't forth-coming with any information."

He shakes his head as he continues. "Jeffery Early, the umpire, though did have something to say."

I can't help it, I nod my head because I certainly remember him looking down at Raleigh.

"From what you've said in the locker room, what Mr. Early has said, and from what the video shows—we have decided to release Mr. Raleigh from the team in light of serious team ethics and code violations."

He looks at me for a long moment then gives me a warmer smile. "We just wanted to make sure your arm was well after that throw last night and to make sure you know we look after our players."

I nod my head and fight the urge to roll my throwing arm's shoulder. I don't feel the twinge but just talking about last night creates a ball of dread in the pit of my stomach. I look to Jim who is nodding his head at me.

"Thank you, sir, I appreciated the sentiment."

Art stands up and I rise with him. I shake his hand as he wishes me good day off.

I head over to the locker room and see it is nearly empty except for David Miller, our other catcher.

"David, how's it going, brother?" I ask as I walk up to him and give him the arm grab hug thing we all do.

"Pretty good. Looks like you guys had an interesting morning already," he says as he points to Raleigh's empty locker.

Even the name tag is missing.

I nod my head and say quietly in the empty room, "Yeah, it looks like he did tell Suarez which pitch I was going to throw last night. They released him already."

Shaking his head, David sighs, "What a stupid fucking kid."

He's right, I think. David is hitting forty next year and has already announced his retirement. He's pretty much the old man in the clubhouse, and we all listen to his advice. He's been around long enough to know what's what.

"Any idea who they are going to bring up?" I ask him. I sure hope whichever minor we have will be a good match for the team.

"Not sure yet, but if I hear anything I will let you know."

Nodding, I move on and drop my stuff at my locker then change into my workout gear.

I stop first at the physical trainer's office to go through a post-game checkup before heading to the gym for a very thorough workout. I have a lot of steam built up inside my muscles.

Raleigh and Clarissa have me pushing it hard for a solid hour.

I am a sweaty, dripping mess before I finally shower

and sink myself into a sauna. This, more than the weights, helps my body finally relax.

Other guys filter through the clubhouse throughout the morning and stop to talk to me a bit. Beyond Raleigh, I'm friends with every guy here. I have no clue why the fucker had such a huge fucking chip on his shoulder. There wasn't a need for it. We are a damn good team. His cockiness was just annoying and overdone.

Well, I may have fucked his sister at a Christmas party two years ago, but to be fair, I had absolutely no clue she was his sister or that she was engaged to some guy at the time. Fuck, it wasn't my fault, she threw herself at me and as any responsible person I caught her.

Walking out of the building and towards my car, I see a baseball bat slamming into my taillight before I see the man swinging it. Raleigh is standing there in a hitting stance as he takes a swing at the rear window.

What the fuck?

I grab my phone and dial the cops as I charge over to him.

A couple of the other guys are right behind me and I can hear their shouts as I yell, "What the fuck are you doing, shithead?!"

Raleigh stops hitting the car and looks at me. His eyes are full of rage as he screams, "You got me fired!"

Dropping the bat, he runs at me and is all fists as he tries to beat me into a pulp.

Thank fuck I have height and weight on the fucker because I don't hold back as I throw one giant fucking punch to his chin. His head snaps back as he crumples to the ground.

"Fuck!" I yell out as I pull my hand close to my body. That fucking hurts!

The alarm on my nightstand is the devil, I absolutely swear it. It rings at me five times a week, every week. It never lets me sleep in, and if I try it, only screams at me ten minutes later.

I push myself up, out of the covers, and glance at the clock. It's only 1 p.m. but I have a shift in an hour. Tony was good about my request to be on a new shift.

I just didn't expect him to put me on it the very next day.

I'm *so* tired. I got home at seven, kissed grandma good morning and went straight to bed. Going to bed didn't mean I fell asleep though.

How could I when all I could think about was that giant asshole almost kissing me?

Ugh! I don't even like the guy, yet I can't stop thinking about him.

Can't stop thinking about his gorgeous blue eyes or those bulging arms crossed over his massive chest.

The way his lips curved as he smirked cockily at me.

I'll see you again soon, he promised me.

And I just stood there like an idiot.

I make a disgusted sound in my throat. What is wrong with me? Why do I feel like I'm going boy crazy?

Shaking my head, I try to get myself together. If I want to get to work on time and keep my shift I need to get my butt moving now.

The shower helps clear my head, and the coffee my grandmother has waiting for me when I step into the kitchen is exactly what I need.

Oh my god, I love coffee today. I have a feeling that coffee will be my best friend the next couple of days as I get used to this new schedule.

Grandma is talking to me as I sit down at the table, nibbling on a couple pieces of toast before I run out the door and drive to work.

She clears her throat loudly and asks, "Sweetheart, are you even paying attention?"

"Huh?" I ask and blink.

Somehow my thoughts were wandering again... Thinking about a tight ass in designer jeans.

"I was asking how your night went last night?"

Shrugging my shoulders, I say, "Not bad, slow as usual..."

I can't help but trail off as I think about the guy and how his beard would feel if he kissed me. I bet it would tickle my cheeks.

Oh, jeeze. I so need to get my head out of the clouds. He was such a cocky ass, I would never date a guy like him. Too cocky, too pushy and way too out of my league in looks.

I'm nothing special to look at. Strawberry blonde hair, pale skin and too thick for my own tastes. A guy like him... he was probably only interested in me because I was the only girl available and he was drunk.

"Clarissa, honey, you are staring off into space like you live there. Do you think maybe you should start your new shift tomorrow?"

With a shake of my head, I sigh. "No... I'm okay. I was just thinking of a customer last night."

I look down to my toast and the newspaper sitting on the kitchen table.

The sports page is already wrinkled and creased in places from where grandma has been looking up news on her beloved Stars.

Sometimes I think she loves them more than anything else. She's been a fan of theirs since they came out to California in the 60's, and hasn't lost her love for the team since. They haven't had a lot of luck the last couple of years, but she sure hasn't allowed that to stop her rooting for them with all her heart.

I flip the pages a couple of times as I nibble on my toast and check to see how they did last night.

"Holy shit!" I squeak out loudly.

"Clarissa!" Grandma admonishes me.

"*Oh. My. God.*" My eyes widen further as I stare at the page.

I blink a couple of times before I'm sure I'm not hallucinating from lack of sleep.

Staring at the page, I reread the headline: 'JACKSON STRIKES 'EM OUT!'

I read the article, but there's very little written about the giant man on the page.

The cameraman snapped the picture of him when he was mid-throw. His face a mask of pure intensity as he throws the ball as hard as he can. His muscles are bulging in his arm, his beard all bushy and almost caveman like.

He looks like he could club a girl over the head and drag her back to his cave.

I doubt very much he'd have to resort to that. I'm quite sure girls would willingly throw themselves at him. No clubbing needed. Well, maybe the club between his...

Shit, quit thinking about that.

I mutter to grandma, "You say lots worse when you are watching... Him."

My finger points at the chest of Jackson Crass on the paper and I wonder what it would be like to touch that magnificent chest.

"Well..." she laughs quietly. "I suppose I do. He is quite fetching, though, isn't he?"

I nod my head to her and stare for a couple more seconds. Holy cow he is good looking. Especially with those blue eyes that stared into my own last night... they were so deep and beautiful. His jet-black hair and beard makes such a striking contrast.

Oh, god. It *has* to be a different guy.

Last night could *not* have been this sculpted, mouth-watering example of male perfection.

Looking up to the clock, I check the time and stand quickly.

Grabbing my purse, I give grandma a kiss on the check. "Love you, I will see you tonight. Will you be okay for dinner?"

She gives another laugh. "Dear, I will be just fine."

Shooting out the door, I hop in my car, shaking my head.

There is no way the man from last night could be the same guy in the paper...

It can't be for one reason alone—a guy like that would never be interested in a boring girl like me.

CHAPTER FIVE
JACKSON

Sitting here in the hospital with my hand under an x-ray is not how I thought I would be spending the rest of my day.

I highly doubt I broke anything, but when I initially hit Raleigh I did feel some pain.

Damn. Punch lit up my hand like a motherfucker.

Cops questioned me a bit, but with all the witnesses, and the footage from the security cameras, I was deemed to be in the right... so far.

I guess, in theory, he could try to sue me, but for what? Getting his ass knocked out after he damaged my car? No clue, but fuck him.

Jim, of course, came flying out of the building as soon as he heard, and even Art made an appearance. Art told the cops he wanted to pursue a trespass with Raleigh, and Raleigh is no longer permitted on the property.

That's good for us, bad for him. Raleigh is now not allowed on a baseball team's property. If he gets picked up by another team, odds are he will be forced to miss at least a few games.

"How's it going besides the hand, Jackson?" Doctor Sadana asks.

"Not so bad," I say as I try flexing my sore hand. It hurts, but not like it did at first.

"Good, good. I don't see any broken bones or fractures. You will have some swelling and soreness but that should go away over the next day or so. I want you to ice it, and if you feel anything beyond the pain you are feeling right now, you call me on my cell? Got it?"

Nodding my head, he shakes my left hand and then exits the room.

A nurse walks through the door as soon as he leaves and smiles at me. She is a little cutie—blonde, thin and has big tits. More than likely, though, the blonde is as fake as her tits.

A bright white smile goes with the rest of her. She must be bleaching the shit out of her teeth. "Hey big guy, you ready to go home?"

Nodding my head, I stand up from the chair. Tilting my head to the side, I hear a loud pop. God, that felt good. "Yep."

She smiles as she looks up into my eyes. "Want some help down to your car?"

Internally I wince. Yeah, she is looking to get some star sauce in her.

Shaking my head, I turn her down gently. "Nah, I got it."

I walk out of the room without looking back. The team will take care of everything else, and I seriously don't need the Barbie doll back there tagging along.

Red is on my mind anyways. Damn girl was sexy as fuck last night. My cock stiffens just a bit at the thought of her juicy ass as she walked away. If I could have, I would have bit it right then and there. It's an ass that just begs to be slapped hard. To be spanked for the sole purpose of spanking it, to see it bright red.

Fuck me, I want to spank her ass right now then slam my cock into her tight pussy.

Just thinking of Clarissa has my tongue wetting my lips, I bet that pussy tastes good as fuck.

One of the team drivers is waiting for me at the entrance of the hospital along with an athletic trainer from the team. The trainer wraps an ice bag around my right hand and then passes me a couple of Advil and an opened bottle of water.

"Where to Mr. Crass?" The driver asks.

"Back to the stadium, I need to get my car."

"Yes, sir, though I can drive you home if you want and have your car delivered there if you would like."

I make a fist with my hand and give it a squeeze—not much pain.

"Yeah, let's do that... Wait... actually... do you know of a good repairman for my car? It got fucked up with a baseball bat."

"Yes sir, I can have it delivered there if you would like."

"Yeah, do that." I reach forward and put my car keys into his hand.

I lean back into the seat and let my mind blank out for a bit.

I need to relax. The whole shit from last night has me tense and this morning sure as hell didn't make it any better. Asshole has trashed my fucking car. Bet my insurance company will like that shit. Fuck, it's only five months old.

"Motherfucker," I grumble at the thought of all the shit Raleigh has caused because he was being a big fucking baby.

It's not like I knocked up his sister, for fucks sake. Shit, she told me I could go bareback, but fuck that shit.

"Sir?" the driver asks and the trainer turns around from the front seat.

"Nothing, guys, just thinking about the asshole who fucked my car up. Same stupid fuck who I hit this morning."

"Ah, okay, sir. That sucks."

Nodding my head, I continue to grumble but not out loud.

Pulling my phone out of my pocket, I quickly check it. The damn thing blew up while I was in the hospital. My agent, Jim, and the guys from the team.

Fuck, this is going to be annoying. I bet the press is going to want a piece of this. Shit.

Fuck. Fuck. Fuck. We are on a long home game stretch. This is going to fucking suck. They will be asking all kinds of questions, wanting to know all the dirty details.

I call Jim back first. "Hey, shit's good with my hand. No brakes or fractures."

"That's great news!" I can hear the smile in his voice when he says that. I'm our number one pitcher, there's a lot riding on me.

"Yeah, I got a call from Colt already... So it's been leaked to the press?" I ask.

"Yeah, we got a call from ESPN already for comments. We've chosen to play it quiet until we know what's up with your hand."

"How does the team want to handle this?"

"So far, it will be, we released Raleigh this morning and there was a disturbance in the parking lot, but we have no comment."

"Nice. I'll be going with that myself. I'll call Colt."

"Sounds good with me," he says.

"Jim, am I in any trouble with Art? I really don't want..."

He quickly talks over me. "Not at all, Jackson. He is happy with you and has no problems. He is working on a possible trade before the deadline to get us a good hitting catcher. I don't know what he has in the works, but he came to talk to me for a bit a while ago and said we would be in fine shape soon."

"Hmph, that sounds good to me." I say.

Art is a genius when it comes to getting what he wants from his players. Thanks to him, and some deep pockets, we are now a winning franchise and a winning team. It wasn't always so...

Our organization has consistently been called cocky, self-assured and arrogant. When it was brought up in an interview with Art, he just laughed about it and said we sure as hell are.

We have that winning mentality now. This is our year to break through the barrier and win the World Championship. We are on track to be champions and it makes me a happy fucking camper.

I fucking hate to lose.

"One thing, though, Jackson," Jim says and his voice

isn't as happy. "We want you to take off the rotation for two to three games."

"Am I being punished?"

"No. I know it feels like it but I want you rested up. We are close to the end and I cannot afford for you to go down to a hand or shoulder injury. I watched you last night and this morning. You have been rolling that shoulder."

Fuck. He's right of course, but I'm not injured… just a little twisted up.

"Shit."

"Don't worry, Jackson, you've got about a fifteen-day vacation. Go get some sun and relax. I've already talked to the pitching coaches and trainers. They all agree. Even Art said it's a good idea."

"You think this will make me look guilty of something?"

"No. Art is already spinning it to look like you're resting up for the big push this season. Damn genius that he is."

We don't say much more; I don't want the vacation but it will do me some good, I think. I will still be throwing to keep in shape and warmed up, but not attending the games. Shit.

Disconnecting the call, I dial up my agent. "Hey Colt, what's up?"

"Shouldn't I be asking you the same thing? News is you were in the hospital this morning, and that there was a brawl outside the stadium and that you were a part of Raleigh leaving."

Well, fuck me, he is informed.

"Yes, yes, and no."

"Okay... how do you want me to spin this?"

"No comment is where the team will go."

"Shit. That just makes them harass me all the more, Crass."

"I know, but it's what they are doing so I will be too."

"So you wanna talk about what's going on?"

"Nah, I think I'm good. Art is happy with me and Jim is too."

"Okay, if that changes, let me know the instant you know. If I hear anything, I will as well."

"Thanks, Colt."

"It's what you pay me for."

We hang up and I think about what he said. He's right, though, it's what I pay him a shit ton of money for. He isn't there to massage my ego, he is there to protect me and keep me working. I actually like the guy though, he doesn't lie to me and he always goes for the highest dollar amount for me. What's not to love?

The calls from the guys are thankfully quicker. All are happy Raleigh is gone and some want to go out and get wasted as soon as we can. Might be a good idea.

I take a nap as soon as I get home. The a/c in the house is like a fucking refrigerator and I absolutely love it. My body and mind are tired as I lay down on the mattress. My cock is still unhappy about not having Clarissa with me, but I figure it's only a matter of time before I make her mine.

Holy cow, I slept the whole night through. I didn't wake once.

That's a good thing because right before I did pass out I was thinking about the guy from the diner and how I had to be wrong. No way was he the same guy in the paper. He has the same eyes of course and the same kind of beard... But those beards are so damn trendy right now it doesn't mean a thing.

Checking the clock, it's closer to nine than it is eight.

I smile in happiness.

I haven't slept this solidly for some time and it feels good. I want to lay here for the rest of the day, to feel the warmth of the blankets and sheets wrapped around me. But no, I can't. The smell of bacon is calling to me.

"Hello there, sleepyhead. How was your first night off third shift?" Grandma asks me as I come into the kitchen.

"Really good. I slept like a log, but it's not going to last. I think it was only because I was so dead tired last night."

"I remember when your grandfather went from third to first shift. It took him a couple of days to get used to it."

"I bet it was tough for him. What did he think of the people he chased after on first shift? Was it different than third?" Grandpa was a police officer for the Los Angeles police department. He was a very stern man when it came to things, but deep down he was a gigantic teddy bear of a person.

"He said there were more drunks at night than during the days, but he saw more of the nasty bad guys during the day."

He was a good person; strong, smart and very caring. The car wreck that took his life almost took grandma with him. She wasn't in the car but it didn't matter—she lost her one and only true love.

"Do you think he would have been better off staying on third shift?" I ask.

"No. He was tired of nights and not getting to see us. He hated that most of your childhood and teens were spent with him being away or sleeping."

"Yeah..." I say and I feel a little sad at the thought. I sure missed him during those years, and when he was finally able to fully be in my life he was there for only a couple of years. It wasn't fair.

"Cheer up, Clarissa. He's still here watching over us," Grandma says as she reaches over the kitchen table and grasps my hand.

I smile and nod my head.

"Can't be away from his favorite girls, right?"

"Nope," Grandma says.

Quietly eating breakfast, I'm reading through the website of the college I plan on enrolling in, checking out their creative writing classes while Grandma is watching the sports channel on TV.

"Oh, dear!" I hear her exclaim as I am checking up on how to reenroll.

"What's wrong?"

"They released Jeff Raleigh. There was a fight at the stadium, and Jackson was seen at the hospital!"

"What?" I ask, confused about what she's talking about.

I only truly understand that Jackson was seen at a hospital—my visitor at the diner's twin brother.

"Well, that's just... the... the sports caster doesn't even say anything about what's happening. How useless is that?" she asks as she stands up from the table and takes her plates to the sink.

She is muttering about poor journalism as she heads to the living room and switches off the TV.

I smile and shake my head. "Sorry to hear that about your Stars, Grandma."

"Our Stars, young lady. I don't allow any non-fans in my home."

Laughing, I head back to my room to get dressed for the day.

***

"Hey, Clarissa!" Amanda calls out cheerfully as I walk into the diner.

It's definitely a different way to walk into work. Usually on third I get a tired greeting from the staff and that's about it. Second shift seems to be much happier, and perkier.

I wave back and head into the tiny break room. Storing my purse and getting ready, I head out into the diner and look at all the people sitting there. It isn't busy just yet, but I know it will be soon enough.

I head to the side of the diner bar and look for which tables I will be serving tonight when Amanda gives me a hip bump. "Hey, honey? What ya doing?"

Glancing at the paper, I see it's the same as last night. "Just getting ready. Why?"

"Cause I thought you'd be helping that guy who has been waiting for you. Damn, he is fine!"

I look to my section and let out a small groan.

Shit.

I stand still, frozen to the spot. I'm not easily shocked or speechless, but seeing him sitting there leaves me stunned stupid. Inwardly I'm slamming my head into a wall. I want to do anything but just stand here. I need to move, but his damn cocky grin has me stopped dead in my tracks.

Move, you silly girl, I say to myself.

Amanda hips me again and I am suddenly moving towards the table on autopilot or something because I certainly have no control over my feet.

He is still so very handsome and in person, in high definition he looks entirely too much like that guy in the sports section.

"Afternoon, Clarissa? You didn't switch shifts because of me, did you?" he asks.

He isn't smiling now.

"No... Classes are... I'm reenrolling," I stammer out.

What the hell is wrong with me? Why is my brain

fuzzy? And why is my heart pounding like I've been running a marathon?

He grins at me. "So what time do you get off tonight? I tried seeing you last night but you were already gone?"

Finally, my brain kicks in. "What's your name, again?"

"Jackson. Ever heard of me?"

Oh, fuck, it really is him.

"You so need to leave... Grandma will kill me if she finds out I said that..." I say and mentally slap myself.

His eyebrows quirk up as he asks, "Huh?"

"Look, I don't like guys like you.... You're not my type... Go away." I whisper loudly to him.

I don't want to get in trouble for being so rude to a customer.

"Nah, I haven't even eaten yet," he says like I didn't even say anything about not liking him.

I grind my teeth together and ask, "What would you like to eat, sir?"

"I'll have my usual, Clarissa," he smirks.

Fucker actually smirks at me.

"Your usual?" I ask, "You have only been here once."

"Yep, but I bet you know what it is..." he says as he trails off.

His eyes roam down my body and then back up to my face. He is figuratively taking my clothes off in his mind, I can just tell it. He is stripping me naked. The fucking asshole.

"I don't..." I start to say, but he's right.

I do.

Two steaks and fries, large tea. Gah.

Stomping away, I head to the kitchen window to place the order. I know he is watching me walk away and I can't help how my ass sways. It just does. I swear, I'm not trying. Honest.

JACKSON

I don't know if that ass sway is intentional or not, and I sure don't care. Her ass is a thing of beauty.

And those hips of hers make me want to grab 'em and fuck the strawberry out of her hair.

I look down at my crotch and try not to smirk, even my big boy down there wants a piece of her.

Clarissa looks pretty damn irritated that I am here for her, but that's not my concern. She will come around for me, I just know it. I can't even remember the last time I didn't get the girl. I don't think it's ever happened before.

My steaks are cooked as well as they can be in place like this, but they will do. Since she seems to be playing hide and peek with me, I pull out my phone and scroll through my texts, checking to see if anyone needs me for anything.

I am not exactly comfortable with this whole situation or with the team's decision to release Raleigh. Right now, I hate the fucker for the problems he's caused, but it also puts me in a bad light because immediately after he gets released, I'm spotted in a hospital and taken off throwing rotation.

None of it looks good. Especially because it's not often a guy gets released like he did. If anyone checks into the police reports they will see the trespass report on him as well. Yeah, it looks bad on him, but it could make me look like a primadonna.

I've worked damn hard to get to the spot I am in right

now. I'm thirty years old and I sure as fuck have worked my ass off. I don't need the shit he was pulling.

I have no doubt the whisper mill through the league is already running full steam. Pulling a stunt like he did with telling the batter what I was going to throw is a pretty big fucking issue, but going psycho on my car is beyond how someone should act. I have never seen someone fucking lose his shit like that.

My steaks are done and the fries are just about gone as Clarissa sweeps by, taking my nearly full glass of tea away to refill it.

I wish she would stop moving for just one moment though. I need to talk to her ass but she is doing her damnedest to get away from me.

No more of this avoidance thing.

She walks by me with a glass and tries to set it down and go.

I pride myself with how fast I am. As soon as the glass touches the table, I grab her hand and pull her down into my booth with me.

She lets out a squeak of surprise as her hips bumps into mine. Her wide eyes turn towards me and she starts to pull herself back up from the booth.

I pull her wrist down again and say, "If you don't sit down I will make sure everyone sees me kissing you goodbye."

She glances around at all the people staring and blushes deeply.

Her red flushed cheeks don't mask the anger that quickly flares up. She whispers hotly, "You can't just kiss someone whenever you want!"

Grinning at her, "You're right, I can't."

"So you..." she starts to say.

Not letting her finish, "But I can with you."

Again, her cheeks redden as I go on. "Now before I get going, tell me what time you get off."

"No chance, creep."

I motion to another waitress to come over and I can see Clarissa is practically buzzing on my lap with aggravation, but I'll be damned if I don't smell one of the sexiest scents from her I have ever smelled.

She smells like a woman and sex rolled into a batch of lilacs.

Fuck, she smells so good I am getting poetic. That's fucked up.

The brunette waitress—wearing a name tag that reads: Amanda—comes over, grinning. Clarissa is staring daggers at me but I can tell she wants me anyways. All chicks do.

"Amanda, what time do you guys get off?"

Grinning widely, she's quick to say, "Depends on how well you do your job."

Snickering, I look down to Clarissa. She has started sinking down into the booth.

Clarissa mutters, "Someone please save me."

"Now, now. I get the feeling our little Clarissa is easily embarrassed."

"True. She gets off at ten-thirty."

I smile and Amanda starts to turn away before turning back to say, "If she doesn't want to go out with you, I sure will."

"Please take her!" Clarissa says next to me. I smile and shake my head.

Amanda strolls away as I look down at my strawberry blonde girl. She is bright red, and it's fucking beautiful.

But I want to see her flushed for other reasons. I want to see her spread out across my Egyptian cotton sheets, her skin flushed with desire and her arms reaching for me.

Sitting up straight she moves to get out of the booth and I let her.

"See you at ten, sweetcheeks," I grin.

"Over my dead body," she snaps back before slapping my check on the table. I drop another hundred on the bill and stand up from the booth.

The register girl smiles at me as I walk towards the door. "Sir... You need to pay."

"I already did, it's on the table."

"Oh. Well, have a good night."

"One thing, though. Clarissa asked me to drop something off in her car, but I forgot which one it is..."

"Oh, she drives that black Escape over there."

"Thanks."

Nodding, I head out to my motorcycle. I thrum the engine a couple of times to get it warmed up. She's a loud bike but she is all mine. I love the way she rumbles as I pull out of the parking lot and head out to the city.

The driver yesterday took my car to the shop and I want to go talk to them and see what all can be done.

It's a bit of a drive to get to the other side of the city but I make pretty good time on the bike. Pulling into the lot, I see my Lexus in one of the bay doors. It is beat to hell and back.

Raleigh did a pretty big number on my car. The windows are all smashed in, the headlights are destroyed, and the engine hood looks like it has fallen down a mountain. The tires are all flat too.

Fuck.

I look around the car more and I see dents everywhere.

Shit.

I get off the bike and head into the office. A small guy comes up to me and asks, "How can I help ya?"

"I'm here about the Lexus."

"Ah, yeah. Brian had that towed over to me. It's sure beat to hell and back. You piss off some broad's brother or somethin'?"

Chuckling, I say. "Something like that. Is it all cosmetic or did he do any permanent damage?"

"It's all cosmetic so far except for the tires. Those are wasted. They were knifed to shit. Those dents though will be a bitch to get out. I might have to replace some stuff if I can't pull 'em."

Motherfucker, I haven't even put fifteen thousand miles on the car and it's already trashed.

Sighing, I say, "See what you can do and call me. Let me know, though, before anything is done."

My mood is definitely not good. Fuck. I am going to need a long workout now.

He is one-hundred percent ass!

And if he didn't look or smell so damn good I would have slapped him.

Pow! Right in those kissable lips.

I bet they would feel so good to kiss too. How the hell am I thinking about that? Damn, he really needs to not be so sexy. He needs to get out of my head.

The way he watched me when I was working was maddening. He watched me like a lion does a gazelle. My legs, my ass. My face and lips. It was like each part of me was closely observed and filed away as something he would be using later.

I wouldn't really slap him though... I don't have that kind of nerve.

In my head, I may bonk the crap out of him, but in real life I'd just give him a really mean snarl. If I could growl at him I would. I don't think that would help though.

He'd probably just think of it as some weird ass foreplay.

That he would even dare pull me down beside him was completely beyond my comfort zone. That asshole was acting like some weird romance book lover or something. Those guys my grandma fawns over—all big, alpha and cocky. I don't do cocky guys...

Well, that may be a problem. I don't do non-cocky either. I don't do guys, period. I suppose I've been on this self-imposed celibacy for too long.

I tried the whole intimacy thing once, and it sucked way too much. Well, I mean... even now it gets me angry. He was one of those guys who got everything he could from me and then bolted. When I finally gave in and stupidly gave my virginity to him, he told everyone in school.

I have never been so damn embarrassed in my life.

Grandpa being a cop though, yeah... I told Grandma what happened, promising her to secrecy and next thing I know Grandpa went to the guy's house and requested he come over to my house to offer a full apology.

Yeah, that helped... not.

But Grandpa was like that, fiercely protective of his girls. I've never seen someone since him love like he did us. His heart was built for us two. When I think about possibly dating or giving a relationship a shot, I think of Grandpa and how he looked at Grandma. Maybe because of them I put love on too high of a pedestal.

I hold all men to his standard.

I don't see Mr. Arrogant walk out the door, but when I get to the table I see another hundred laying there. Butthead! How dare he just tip me like that? I'm not going to be giving him any extra favors, if that's what he thinks!

Next time, I am telling the cook to burn his steak. That's if he dares show his face in here again.

Thankfully the rest of my shift goes smoothly. I am tired as can be but there are a lot more customers coming in and they aren't drunk like the third shift crowd. Tips are pretty good, good enough that if things keep going this way I might be able to swing getting into classes next semester, and that would be totally awesome.

I want to get back into school so bad. I want to do more with my life, I want more for myself. I don't think less of anyone who sticks with being a waitress but it's not my calling. I don't know what is, but I want to find out.

I don't see Mr. Cocky, though, waiting for me when my shift ends and just the smallest part of me is disappointed he didn't have the follow through.

To hell with him.

I wave goodbye to everyone.

Letting out a sigh of exhaustion, I walk out the door and look to where my little Escape is. It was Grandpa's home car and Grandma told me to keep it so it would be used and not wasted. She has her monster Excursion. They bought that big SUV right around graduation time, and she looks entirely too small in that big thing but she loves it.

I tried driving it once and nearly ran over three different cars. Big vehicles and I do not match.

Well, crap. I don't match with motorcycles either.

There he is, Mr. Giant. Wearing a black t-shirt, tight fitting blue jeans and black boots. Leaning against a big motorcycle.

The motorcycle looks loud and very dangerous. I can feel my jaw drop and I'm gawking at him. If I were into the whole total bad-boy look I would so be drooling over him right now. I mean, he's so not the reason my nipples just tightened and a little zip of excitement went straight to my un-used lady bits.

"What are you doing?" I finally ask as I walk towards my car.

He is parked right next to me and I will have to walk near him to get to my car. It's so unfair.

"I told you I would see you after you got off of work," he says.

And right now I'm debating which is more deep and gravelly, his voice or the bike?

He's actually grinning, dammit. I want to call him a bunch of rude names but I settle with, "Go away. I am soooo not the girl you are looking for."

"Well, I think you are the droid I am looking for."

"Huh?" I stammer. I mean I know he just made a Star Wars reference, but it kinda caught me off guard.

"Never mind. Anyways, what do you feel like eating for dinner?"

With a shake of my head, I shut him down. "I already had dinner."

"Liar."

My cheeks feel hot. I am so over this guy. I walk right up to him. He is leaning against his bike, but damn, he is still taller than me.

"Stop that." I say and can't help it. I am pointing my

finger at him like he's a naughty child or something.

I feel so absurd that I am in this position but I can't help it. He's just too cocky. Too assured that I want him when I've tried my best to give him the impression I'm *not* impressed or interested.

He crosses his arms across his chest and I can't help but notice how the muscles roll and shift together. Those arms are big, like... *me Tarzan, you Jane big*. He could throw me over his shoulder and take me anywhere.

I doubt it wouldn't take him any effort at all to lift my curvy butt up.

"Stop what?" he asks and he is acting quite serious, but I can see the smile behind his big bushy beard. I think beards like his are absurd. What is this? A throwback to the eighteen-nineties?

"Stop calling me out on things and quit being so damn self-assured! It's absurd!"

He frowns at me. "I'm not self-assured..."

"Oh yes, you are, and... and... Oh yeah, don't go threatening to kiss me either! I am not your girlfriend or anything else."

He smirks again. "I didn't say you were. If you were my girlfriend, I would have slapped that sexy ass you were swaying in my face back in there."

Will my cheeks ever not be red? I swear being a redhead is a curse. "It's not sexy and you most certainly will not be doing that, either."

Shaking his head, he says, "Clarissa, let's start over again. You really seem to not understand my intentions."

"And I don't want to! I don't have time for your kind of ...*intentions*." I am not sure why I say it the way I do, but I make the word sound dirty at the end.

I don't have time for this guy. School and work. Those are going to be my main focuses. Maybe some time in the future find a nice, quiet guy who doesn't go assuming all kinds of things.

A nice, quiet boring guy who doesn't look at me like he wants to tear all my clothes off with his big, strong hands and have his way with me right now and right here, regardless of who's watching.

"I am fairly sure you are going to like my intentions," he says, standing from the bike.

My hand slowly falls to my side as he looks down at me. And I tell myself in my head my future guy will be much smaller. Too big like this is just... well, I don't want to tell myself what it is.

I don't say anything. I just stare up at him, trying to look as sure as the words that came out of my mouth.

"I'll make you a bet, Clarissa."

"What kind of bet?"

I have to lick my lips for some reason. They are all of a sudden dry and feel like they need to be moistened.

"I'm going to kiss you, and if you tell me to go away afterwards, I will."

"No," I say.

"No? No, what?"

"No kissing, that's not fighting fair."

I'm staring at is lips right now. I can see them beneath his beard. They look full and very, very unfair.

Leaning down, he approaches my mouth with his.

I tell myself to be clinical and cold about this. To not give in. It's just two orifices opening for one another.

His tongue is too wet, he is too pushy, he is taking advantage of me.

Yeah, right... none of those things are true.

The kiss is like lightning.

I'm so stunned at first I don't do anything. Then he gently pushes his tongue past my barrier and it's like someone flipped a switch. My floodgates open and the kiss that is making my head swim with arousal is sending all kinds of delicious jolts dancing across my skin.

I really have no clue how long we kiss, but somehow my right hand is gripping the chest of his shirt like a mad woman. He has one hand on my cheek and the other in my hair.

He is a kissing machine, I swear to god.

Crap! I slowly slide my hand away from his very muscular ass. It really is a delicious, muscled ass, and I so hope he didn't notice my hand was there.

Pulling back, I feel like my world is tilting and quickly try to get my bearings back. "How... How..." I stammer.

"How, what?" he rasps out. Peering into his eyes, they're blazing with the heat of two blue fires.

"How did my leg get wrapped around you? Did you do that?"

I have no clue how my leg got wrapped around his like that.

"No, darling, that was completely you. So was the hand on my magnificent ass."

I would poke his chest for that, but he's right, it is magnificent.

Thank god, for work panties right now, because I have a serious case of over-heating down there.

I pull myself away from him and those large, warm hands.

"That didn't prove anything," I say dismissively,

wanting desperately to believe it.

"You're lying again, Clarissa." he says to me, and then laughs merrily.

He has a really good laugh.

"Shut it. Let me have my illusions."

"Nope. So where do you want to go to eat? Or do you want to get a drink?"

I think for a moment and I'm so tempted to just throw caution to wind. "I can't. I have to go check on my Grandma."

He shrugs his shoulders and says, "Okay, think she's hungry?"

I look up at him with disbelief and he shrugs again. "What?"

"You can't come with me! She would... she would have a heart attack!"

"You don't know that... Old women love me. *Love me.*"

"That's... that's...What?" I ask.

"Old women love me, and little kids. I am really good with both."

"I... Damn... You're just going to follow me anyways, aren't you?"

"Yeah, after that kiss? Clarissa you won't be getting rid of me easily."

With that sort of kiss, I'm lucky I'm not pregnant.

I don't say that to him, though, because I'm not sure how much I can control myself with someone who can kiss me like the world is ending.

I climb in my car and he backs his bike out of the spot next to mine, I just about have a heart attack when he starts that thing up and revs it.

That thing is loud and sounds like one giant roar.

So this chick wraps herself around my body like a silk glove and then asks me how her leg did that.

Shit, she was even grabbing my ass!

I do have a pretty good ass if I'm being honest. My body isn't anything to sneeze at either. I put a lot of fucking effort into looking fucking good.

She tasted fucking amazing, though, and even after working a full shift in the diner she smells good.

Somewhere I feel like I might have thought of her as a one-time fling... something to get out of my system.

Yeah, once ain't gonna be enough. I'm going to need at least a week or more with this woman.

Her hands felt so damn good against me. I usually don't go for a chick who's so much shorter but she is breaking all the standards of what I usually go for.

She certainly isn't some shrinking violet. She tells me what she thinks and I like that.

Most of the time I am with some bimbo whose head

is like a bobble head. All nodding and shaking it according to what they think I want to hear.

Someone always saying things I want to hear is annoying.

Following Clarissa home is a new experience for me. I haven't had to pursue a woman in some time. There might be something to that... Maybe she is a woman and I am used to girls?

Well, shit that's a deep thought. Who says all jocks are stupid?

With a shake of my head I focus on the subdivision we turn into.

The streets are nicely kept, from what I can see with my bikes headlights. I don't rev my engine as we slow and turn into a driveway. It's not a large house like mine, but it looks nice and well-kept, like most on the street.

There are lights on in the living room as we come to a stop.

I shut my bike down. Pulling my helmet off my head, I set it down beside the spare I keep for chicks I pick up.

Clarissa gets out of the car and stands there, staring at me as I walk up to her. I shut the door for her and I can tell she is trying really hard to not say something.

"What?"

"Grandma is so going to freak out when you come in the house."

"Nah, she will love me. Old women love me."

She shakes her head at me. "You have no idea what I am talking about."

"Huh?"

Again, another shake of her head and she turns to walk away from me.

I grab her hand before she gets too far.

Twirling her back into my arms, I stare down into those beautiful blue eyes. Leaning down, I close my eyes as I go in for the kiss.

I *need* another taste of her. I need to feel the deep passion she has buried inside of her.

My lips should be touching hers by now, but instead I feel her hand pushing my face away.

"So not going to make out with you in front of my house."

She slips through my arms and starts walking towards the front door.

Glancing over her shoulder, she asks, "You coming?"

I growl quietly under my breath, "Not yet."

Following her to the door, I step into the living room. From behind I see a white-haired lady sitting in front of a large flat screen TV, watching ESPN.

"Clarissa... I swear journalism is just going down the tubes these days. How in the world can they have nothing on the Stars tonight? They won a game and they go into the highlights, but nothing about Crass or Raleigh... Absolutely nothing?"

"Um...Grandma..."

"Seriously, nothing, Clarissa. How am I supposed to know what happened to Crass? Poor thing is in the hospital."

Clarissa is standing there with me, at her grandmother's back, as she's talking about me.

It's actually kinda funny, though, because I get to watch Clarissa turn bright red when her grandmother says, "Even you thought he was pretty darn good looking. I saw you looking at him in the paper."

"Grandma!" Clarissa practically shouts as she stomps her foot.

"Clarissa what is..." the old lady says as she turns around to see me standing there for the first time.

"Hi, ma'am, I'm Jackson. It's nice to meet you," I say as I walk over to her chair, offering her my hand.

Looking from me to Clarissa, and back again, she asks in disbelief, "Are you really..."

Turning my head to Clarissa, "Um..."

"Grandma is the Stars' number one fan, and you are her all-time favorite pitcher."

"Yes, you are," the little lady says to me as I look back to her.

It's my turn to turn start blushing. I am used to fans, but normally I shake hands and keep on moving.

Right now, though, I'm in a fan's house with her granddaughter... who I was trying to violate outside just a few minutes ago.

Clarissa's grandmother looks me up and down as if I am a golden statue she's admiring. "You really are as tall as a giant."

I smirk. Yeah, I'm not a small guy.

"So why are you suspended?" she asks next and it completely catches me off guard.

"Huh? I'm... Why would you think that?"

She motions to the TV and explains, "No one's talking, and all of your fan base is practically abuzz with rumors and gossip. I've been on the internet too, and everyone is trying to figure out what happened."

I sigh. Yeah, I knew the whole tight-lipped, no comment thing would cause some issues.

Looking to her couch, I motion to it, "Mind if I have a seat ma'am?"

"Sure, sure," she says and ushers me over to the couch. She sits next to me and turns. "So what's going on?"

I look over to Clarissa but she is nowhere to be seen. Hopefully she will show back up.

"Promise to keep a secret?" I ask.

Clarissa's grandmother looks just like her, older maybe, but still a beauty. She smiles at me, "I sure will."

Raising my hand, I show her my bruised knuckles. "It's pretty simple. The last game I threw, Raleigh and I had a disagreement."

Okay, so my plan with Jackson is a bit... underhanded on my part, I must admit. I knew exactly what would happen as soon as Grandma saw him, and I've been hiding out in my room for the last twenty minutes. I haven't heard either of them stop talking yet.

I should be honest with myself though. I certainly wouldn't mind kissing Jackson again. I wouldn't mind at all, but I know what it will lead to.

I'd end up in his bed with my legs wrapped around him so tightly he wouldn't be able to pull out. Then, in the morning, I would be shamefully driving myself home after he didn't bother to offer me breakfast.

I don't want that kind of drama in my life, and I don't deserve it.

After that first time with Eric, I was so ashamed that I thought that I was somehow in the wrong, and I just might have deserved what had happened to me.

Slut shaming was horrible in high school. Right or

wrong, it was bad. But when I stood up for myself, it eased off a bit but not much. Kids really can be cruel when they find something and latch onto it.

I knew plenty of girls who got a bad reputation for trusting a boy back then. Moral of the story for me was to keep my legs closed and my brain on. That means no kissing guys.

Especially hot and famous playboy types like Jackson.

But kissing Jackson did very bad things to my resolve.

I'm checking my emails on my phone when I hear Grandma call out not so kindly, "Clarissa, your date is waiting!"

Shit.

Calling right back out, I tell her, "He's so not my date!"

Damn. I feel like I'm fourteen again or something.

"Clarissa, dear, come out here."

Dammit, I'm turning red again.

When Grandma calls me *dear*, it's her way of telling to get my ass moving and do what she wants right now. Last time I tried to ignore the *dear,* she wouldn't make bacon for two weeks straight, and the coffee was always cold.

A girl cannot live on cold coffee and no bacon.

I walk out of my room in an old pair of jeans and a plain white t-shirt. My feet don't even have socks or shoes on. I was so planning on Jackson beating a hasty retreat in the light of Grandma.

No such luck.

"Hey there," Jackson smiles at me.

"Honey, you didn't have to worry about me. A call would have been perfectly suitable to check up on me, though I am not complaining that you brought Mr. Crass here to meet me."

"Yeah, she said you would love to meet me. I couldn't refuse after Clarissa told me how much of a Stars fan you are."

I try really hard not to roll my eyes into the back of my head. He is just so darn smug. "Well..."

"So where are you two going?" Grandma asks.

"Just to get a couple of drinks and maybe a bite to eat," Jackson says easily as if he's had it planned.

"We are?" How dare he even begin to just assume I will go wherever he wants?

"Sure, but you need to put on some shoes or boots. I don't want your feet to get hurt while we're on the bike."

"Wait, what?" I ask but it's like I didn't even speak.

Grandma lights up like a Christmas tree. "Was that your bike I heard?"

"Yes, ma'am."

"Wow, I just love the sound of those loud rumbling bikes," Grandma gushes to Jackson.

And I'm serious, she actually gushes. What the heck?

"I can give you a ride any time you like, ma'am," Jackson says and his smile is just as big as hers.

That's just great. Not only do I have to worry about me dying on his death trap on two wheels but Grandma wants to get on it and take a cruise too.

I start to rub my temples as I feel a giant headache coming on.

"Would you really?" she asks, and I can tell how happy she is. Her eyes are so bright that I find myself smiling.

"Of course! I love my bike. Any chance to ride it is a good time for me."

Shaking my head, I can only imagine Grandma riding on the back of that bike.

Heading back to my room, I grab a pair of running shoes, slide them on quickly, and hope I can get Jackson to understand that while we may be going out tonight, this is a one-time only thing. I'm only doing it to get him out of my hair.

"I like the teddy bear on the bed. Makes me think you aren't nearly as tough as you like to pretend to be." Jackson's deep rumbly voice comes from my doorway.

I can feel my face burning. I'm surprised my hair isn't steaming from how embarrassed I have been getting tonight. Shit.

"You aren't supposed to be back here," I say.

He only grins. "Your Grandmother sent me to get you. I like her. She's pretty spot on with her thoughts about the Stars. She also likes me, probably more than she likes you."

That... asshole!

I grab my teddy bear and throw it where Jackson was but he is already ducking out of the way.

He takes three large steps into my personal space. He's looking around my room and I can't help but feel a little embarrassed. It hasn't changed much since I was fifteen years old. There hasn't been a reason to change it because it's always been just me and Grandma.

I stand up from my bed and try pushing against his chest to get him out of here. All I end up doing is looking silly as he just stands firm, with me pushing on him like some little kid.

His head turns as he slowly takes in my room then he

spots the medals on my walls. "You were a horse rider? Sorry, I don't know the name for it..."

"Kinda. I was a barrel racer for a long time."

"Wow. That's really cool. Why did you say *was*? You stopped?"

I stop pushing at his chest and nod. "Yeah, I just... stopped some time in high school and never went back."

"Just like that?"

I shrug my shoulders. I don't want to go into all the details with him right now. I don't know him well enough. "Yeah."

"That sucks. I couldn't imagine giving up something I'm good enough to get medals in."

Yeah, it sucks, I think but immediately block those memories from my mind and grab his hand. "Let's get going."

Pulling back at my hand, he turns from the medals to me. "Can you teach me how to ride?"

"What?" I blink at him in surprise but he looks completely serious. "Um... maybe."

"No maybes, I want to learn."

"Maybe," I repeat as I start pulling him from my room.

To my relief he comes with me.

We enter the living room and Jackson stops. He gives me a wink and then turns to Grandma. "Ma'am, any chance you can help me persuade Clarissa in teaching me to ride a horse?"

"Of course she will," Grandma says without even a thought. Crap. He used Grandma against me. Double crap.

Heading out of the house, I am torn between being

very aggravated with Jackson for getting his way with Grandma and feeling a pit of dread that we're about to ride this bike somewhere.

"Any chance we can take my car?" I ask as I look up at him.

He took hold of my hand in the living room and hasn't let it go since. I shouldn't like it like but I do, it feels so good.

He even smirks sexily as he looks down at me. "Nope. Not unless I can drive."

I roll my eyes. Okay, sexy is gone. "No."

Standing next to the bike, I raise my eyebrows as he grabs a helmet from the back of his bike and he puts it on my head.

Setting the strap under my chin, he makes sure it is nice and snug.

"Am I a baby now?" I ask.

"Nope, just protecting that beautiful face and head."

I shake my head. "I'm not beautiful."

Looking down at me, he frowns. "Yes, you are."

No, I'm not, I think to his back as he pulls his helmet down.

He stands the bike up and says, "Step on the peg back there and swing your leg over."

I grab onto his back and think of the similarity of a mounting a horse. But that thought is shattered as soon as he starts up this roaring black behemoth.

Holy shit, this bike roars like a lion.

Grandma is standing on the door stoop, smiling and waving as Jackson walks the bike backwards down the driveway. He gets us on the road and at first I just lightly place my hands on his shoulders. I don't know how I should touch him.

"You might want to wrap around me..." he says over the noise from the engine.

"Why?"

He shrugs his shoulders and just goes.

I am pulled from him a moment before I quickly wrap my arms around his waist. Holy shit this thing moves.

We turn a corner and it's a good thing he gave me the warning. Arms tightening around him, I can feel the way he moves and it just feels right being wrapped around him. Especially with the rumbling engine vibrating my thighs. Holy cow. Everything about this feels amazing.

We slow to a stop at a red light and he revs it twice before turning back to me. "Sorry about taking off like that but it's easier to just show it than explain it."

I nod my head at him and clench my teeth shut. Damn, it's been a long time since I have been this horny, and I'm trapped right up against him. Vibrations, being wrapped around his muscular body.

His smell.

He smells like cool air, minty soap, and just *him*.

The way I can feel his stomach muscles under his shirt. It's freakin' torturous.

Crap. I could jump him right here and now.

And he *has* to know the affect all of this is having on me.

We jump forward and head off into the city lights.

He drives us through one of the nicer parts of the city. We stop near a well-lit bar and grill. The rumbling shuts off but I can still feel the vibrations running through me.

He helps me climb off the bike before dropping the kickstand and leaning it. He climbs off, removing his helmet then mine. Thank goodness he is taking care of me, because right now I'm in la-la land.

"Wow," I say and look at him when I finally get my bearings back.

"I take it you like riding my bike with me?"

"Yes." No sense in lying.

He takes me by the hand and leads me over to the door of the building. Inside is a bit louder than I would like, and I think Jackson can tell. He asks the hostess for an outside table.

She takes us outside to a quieter section of tables where the people look like mostly couples enjoying the night. When we get to the table, Jackson walks to a chair and pulls it out for me.

I stand there for a moment like a deer in headlights. The hostess gives me an expectant look, her eyes flicking towards the chair and back to me.

Feeling incredibly silly, I walk up to Jackson and allow him to help me sit. I agreed to come out with him, and regardless of the reasons I just need to go with it.

This has never been done for me before, it's a rather good feeling. It's making me feel like I'm important, and like he cares for me...

Jackson sits down across from me, smiling. "You're beautiful. Don't say you aren't again, not around me."

My head nods of its own accord and I feel a warm, fuzzy feeling in my stomach. I look down at the menu and say quietly, "Okay."

Hearing him call me beautiful is still almost unbeliev-able, but I'll just have to take his word for it.

"So what do you feel like? Drinks and dinner? Or just drinks? Just dinner?"

Looking up from the menu, I smile. "I'm good with both. How about you?"

"Both sounds good," he says as the waitress approaches.

From the menu, I order a gourmet burger and one of those fruity, happy looking drinks. He orders a beer and a burger as well.

When the waitress leaves, it's just the two of us. The other diners are just background, sounds and images off in the distance.

Sitting across from me, giving me his undivided attention, he appears even larger than life. I'm melting under his intense baby blues.

Out of nowhere, says, "Okay, spill it. Why don't you ride anymore?"

I'm caught so off guard by the question I blurt out, "Because I didn't want to be made fun of anymore."

Damn. There goes the moment. I shouldn't have said that but it's the truth. It's stupid and embarrassing too, but it is what it is.

I don't think he was expecting that answer as he takes a moment to digest my answer. "What do you mean? Why would someone tease you about that?"

"It was some stupid bullying in high school," I say and close my mouth.

He leans forward, as if he's truly interested. "That sucks, what happened?"

I shake my head. "I really don't want to talk about it here...Okay?"

I am hoping he will let it drop. I know it's silly to hold

grudges over something that happened back in high school, but I do.

"Okay, I'll drop it for now," he smiles at me, and I like that smile—it's warm and inviting.

He really is a handsome man. Cocky as can be, but handsome. And the way he handled my grandmother is only another point in his favor. I believe I can see through those slimy kind of guys who would try to get into her good graces just to get into my panties.

Jackson wants in my panties for sure, but with Grandma he was being genuine.

He holds my hand across the table and smiles at me. He is so damn good looking. Why in the world would he want me? I'm just your average plain Jane. This is so absurd.

Looking at his hand, I notice there are bruises across his knuckles. I lightly stroke my fingers across his knuckles. "Were you in a fight?"

I hope not. I'm not interested in a hot head who can't control himself. I don't care if he is some superstar.

"Yes, but only in self-defense," he answers.

"What happened?"

"I already told your Grandma, but I really need you both to keep it between us, okay?"

"Okay..."

"Well, did your Grandma happen to mention anything about the team the last few days?"

A lightbulb must appear above my head as I say, "Yeah..."

"Well, what happened is being kept within the clubhouse for the time being, though I have no doubt the story will get out soon enough..."

Jackson is funny and engaging throughout the entire meal. Not only is he polite to the waitress, he also doesn't ogle her breasts even though she keeps shamelessly flaunting in front of him.

I don't have a claim on the guy but I can't help but feel a hint of jealousy at the way she just does it like I'm not sitting right here, across from him.

What is it that keeps his attention on me, and makes her completely dismiss me as a challenge? I don't have giant boobs and I don't look like a plastic Barbie doll, but I'm not disgusting either. My waist probably isn't where it should be for a girl of my height, but I'm not in bad shape. I'm curvy.

I reach over and grab Jackson's hand as the waitress clears our table. I smile at him. She can suck a lemon.

"So..." I start as soon as she's gone. "Why are you hounding me so badly?"

He looks at me for a moment like he's confused then asks, "Hounding you?"

"Yeah, you haven't stopped trying to see me." It's totally scary and kind of flattering, but I want to know why. I don't want to be all bitchy and uptight, but I am so not used to being pursued after stating I'm not interested.

"I don't know how to explain it. There's just something that's special about you. I don't know what it is, but your beauty, your smell, and your attitude are driving me crazy. Crazy enough that I *need* to pursue you."

"To what end? I am not some floozy who is going to just..."

"Floozy?"

"Well... from what I know as soon as you get what you want you will be heading for the nearest exit. Am I right? I mean, your personal life isn't completely private..."

I am not ashamed to admit I googled him a couple of times. Okay, more like quite few times.

He stops at that and I think he gets what I mean. He doesn't say anything for a bit and I quietly watch him mulling over the words we've both said tonight.

"I suppose I should have thought about that. I guess the press and other sites have a lot of information about me?"

I nod my head, it had a lot of information. Like he is a playboy of the highest caliber. He hasn't been spotted with the same woman more than twice.

He shrugs and then says, "Not much I can hide. But I am interested in you. I don't feel like I normally do when I am chasing... I mean dating..."

He mutters something quietly and I swear it sounds like *fuck*.

"So you can see why I am not so sure of your intentions?" I ask, leaning back and crossing my arms over my chest. I need more distance between us.

"Yeah, but that doesn't mean I am going to stop though."

I sigh and nod my head. "I know."

He's already shown how stubborn and persistent he is. I don't know where all of this will lead but I feel like it's getting to the point that I can't fight it. Maybe a small part of me even wants it. There's something between us, despite how hard I'm fighting it. Maybe I should give it a chance?

We stand from the table and I notice that Jackson

leaves a nice but not extravagant tip on the table. I'm flattered but curious now.

As soon as we get to the bike I ask, "Why do you keep leaving me absurd tips?"

Swinging a helmet off the bike, he puts it on my head, "'Cause you're so cute."

I growl but let him snap it on.

Looking over my shoulder as I start up the bike, I ask, "Want to go for a ride?"

"Sure!" she yells over the engine of the bike. "Where do you want to go?"

I look around us and then point to the hills. "How about the hills?"

Nodding her head, she wraps her arms around my waist.

I like how it feels when she does it.

Those full breasts of hers are pushing up against my back, feeling so warm and pliant. I would love to turn around and just bury my face between them. To breathe her in.

I pull the bike out onto the road and head for the hills. I have a couple of parks I know of that I can drive through, and on a night like this it feels great to just ride.

Clarissa being with me on this beautiful night is just a bonus, and it has nothing to do with sex.

Asking me about my motivations, taking in an actual

interest in me, is a point in her favor. She's right about my exploits, even I know how much ammunition I have given to the tabloids. I would like to have told her not to believe the rumors, but I can't. I have truly led the life they show.

Though I have been curtailing it this season.

This season just feels different somehow, it's like the stars are aligning for the team to make it all the way.

At least they were until Raleigh shoved his head up his own ass.

I don't get it; I don't get it at all. Why in the world he would just throw everything we have been working for away is beyond me. Personal differences aside, I seriously have no clue what he is doing or thinking. We are professionals. Shit, what an idiot.

The stars are still up there, though. When I look up into the night sky, I have to squint to see them. All the city lights have dimmed them down. I sure the fuck hope that doesn't happen to the team. We need to burn bright and long to make it all the way.

I will not be a shooting star who just fizzles out.

My emotions are getting to me as I feel myself taking corners a little faster than normal. I am not being reckless but I can tell the way I'm driving has spooked Clarissa. She's holding on to me with a death grip.

I slow my bike as we reach the hills. Here the turns are sometimes long and curvy, and sometimes tight hairpins, but each one gives us the feel of flying.

I don't often let someone ride with me... I know I was acting cavalier with Clarissa and her Grandma but I'm private with the joy riding my bike gives me.

Spotting a lookout on the side of the road ahead, I

slow the bike down to park in one of the carports. Taking our helmets off, we don't talk. The view before us is taking too much of our attention.

The city is laid out before us in a spectacular display of lights.

My hand latches onto hers. Here, I am happy. There are no pressures right now.

I'm not sure how much time has passed but we begin to softly talk to each other. First, it's about the amazing view then it's the nice weather.

I turn to her.

"Clarissa, I need to ask you to ignore all those tabloids and gossip mags. I have been turning over a new leaf. I am not the same man I was last year."

I'm not. I have matured more in the last year than I have in the last ten.

Jim took me aside during the off season and asked where I saw myself in five years. That was a hell of a question to ask me then. We did well last season but just couldn't pull off getting past the post-season.

Actually, we sucked.

And I was a part of the reason we lost. I couldn't put together a winning game to save my life during the wild-card playoffs.

I sucked.

Jim wanted to know where I saw myself, and to me the real question was whether I could produce or should I just be traded off as a mediocre pitcher. Did I want to be the starting ace, or did I want to be just another name in the crowd?

I stopped going out and partying every single night,

then started drinking a shit ton less. Sure, I was still chasing pussy, but I wasn't as avid as I could have been.

I started working out harder and listening to the coaches more. My strength improved, my accuracy and speed went up as well.

I haven't felt this good in years when it comes to health and arm control.

But I still haven't felt the peace I was hoping I could find. Some of the married guys have the *peace* I have been looking for. But shit, I haven't met a single woman in the clubs who could be considered marriage material.

"Why should I? Aren't they true?"

Frowning, I say, "Yes, they are. They're absolutely true. But I'm turning my life around and I don't want to be the same man I was last year."

"What do you mean? Who were you last year?"

"A guy who lost his way. I partied, chased women, worked out only to keep in shape and my arm was turning to shit. I could easily have been traded away and faded from memory. I don't like that. I want to be a better man. A better pitcher. And I want to be a better person."

"Do you really?"

"Yeah."

"Prove it."

CLARISSA

Why in the world did I tell him to prove it? I seriously don't need the distraction right now. I don't... But I can't help it.

Cocky jerk or not, he's growing on me like a fungus. Okay, maybe not a fungus... more like a super sexy leech.

The kiss he gave me earlier still lingers on my lips. That man can suck time out of the night with how he kisses. I don't remember how I ended up with my hand grabbing his ass and my leg wrapped around his. It was like I lost all track of time and my body made decisions without me. I have never been kissed like that, ever.

I want to him to kiss me again, but it doesn't feel right at this moment. There's just something about holding hands and gazing at the city lights that feels... peaceful.

Serene, even.

Driving home is almost anti-climactic. We have much to say to each other, at least I do to him, but it feels like we need to break away for a moment. I need to catch my breath and figure out what the boundaries are.

Do I let myself possibly fall in love with this man? Do I open myself up to that chance? He said he's turning over a new leaf, but I can't hang my heart on his words or empty promises.

It feels like only minutes later and we're pulling in to my neighborhood. I don't know if it's because we were never that far away or if my mind has been so spaced that I didn't pay any attention to where we were going. I've just been enjoying the ride, and the man I'm pressed against.

We sway in sync, my body molded to his back. I know I can sit up a bit more and look around but I don't want to. Here, pressed hard against his back, I can feel the power of his bike as we roar down the streets, and by extension of that I can feel his strength controlling the machine beneath us.

He's warm strength, and sweet, beckoning temptation.

It's all too terrifying to realize how easy it would be to give myself to him.

We pull up in front of my house and come to a complete stop. I loathe getting off this ride, but somehow push my body into action.

I climb off the bike first, and again Jackson takes care of the helmet. I want to be offended that he's presuming that I'll let him take care of me, but I'm not. It's affection, and even if I tell myself I don't need sex, I'm still craving affection.

I stand there as he takes his helmet off, and his hair looks so sexy right now, pushed back and a little wild. Just like him.

He looks down at me and there's this look in his eyes. All the words we want to say are swirling in there. Or maybe it's just what I want to see in them.

Suddenly they spark and light up, reminding me of the stars we just gazed at.

This time I don't try to stop him.

His hands touch my face, touch my hair. He's so gentle, so careful I feel delicate in his hands.

He bends forward, his warmth enveloping me and I hold my breath in anticipation.

His lips part as they meet mine, his tongue invading my mouth slowly, thoroughly.

This time as he kisses me I'm able to keep my senses about me. I'm able to thoroughly appreciate and enjoy every aspect of it.

The way his tongue slides against mine so slowly, so sweetly, easing me into a warm, languid submission.

Then the glide quickens, the strokes pick up, igniting my blood with a new urgency.

My knees go weak and I find myself relying more and more upon his strength to remain standing.

And that was most likely always his intention.

His hands tighten around me and the kiss deepens. His lips are so soft and his beard is tickling my cheeks, but it's his tongue that's driving me wild.

His tongue leads mine into a dance of give and take.

I give and he takes.

Overwhelming me with his sweet taste and all the new, thrilling new sensations.

There's a flash of warmth in my core, like gasoline being thrown on a fire, and I jerk away from him.

I'm panting wildly and all my senses are flooding back.

I need to stay strong.

Deep breath in. *Think for a moment.*

So he's a good kisser... he's had a lot of practice.

I release the breath.

Besides, I don't think Grandma would appreciate it if I tried to take him back to my room so I could have my way with him.

He reaches up and rakes his fingers through his hair. It's even more wild now. "Alright. I want to see you tomorrow..."

His heavy lids lift and he stares me down like he expects me to make a protest.

"I'm off tomorrow," I say softly, my voice sounding wispy and breathless. He grins and I clear my throat. "Come over any time after two."

He walks me to my door and stands there with me on the stoop, grinning at me as I slip inside. "Goodnight Clarissa."

"Goodnight," I croak back.

Once I have the door shut, I lean my forehead against it.

Grandma comes out of her bedroom and stands in the hallway. "You okay, honey?"

Turning from the door, I nod my head. "Yeah, wonderful."

And I am wonderful. I'm just too worked up though for my own good. He was a gentleman, everything I thought I wanted... but I wanted him to be a bad boy and drag me back to his home.

I wanted him to have his way with me.

He didn't though. Why am I so upset about this?

Lying in bed is a miserable affair. Tossing and turning just doesn't seem to help at all.

Does it ever?

The sheets and blanket are rubbing me the wrong way, they are supposed to be warm and snug but right now they are hot and too soft.

Too soft... that's the problem.

I need a big hard body to snuggle up against.

Someone strong and confident. Someone whose very presence breaks through my walls and puts me where I want to be. Where I might *need* to be.

Maybe I do need to break out of this self-protective shell. Shatter all the ties that have been holding me back from experiencing the real world.

Maybe I just need to quit talking to myself and sleep.

Waking up is blissful. I get to wake up when I'm ready, not when the evil alarm goes off. I didn't fall asleep until late last night.

I couldn't get Jackson or his motorcycle off my mind.

That damn rumbling lion between my legs and his hard, muscled body pressed against me.

Damn. Just the memory is getting me hot and bothered.

Rolling out of bed, I pad into the kitchen. Grandma is already sitting there, eating a sandwich and reading the sports page.

"How are the Stars doing without Jackson?" I ask as I pour myself a cup of coffee.

"Good, though he isn't on the pitching rotation. I sure hope he comes back before we go against the Bears. We need his intimidation factor. He scares the socks off them."

We make small talk over a light brunch as I fully wake up. I check the clock on the wall and notice it's only a quarter till noon.

Crap.

I have two whole hours before he might show up. I should have picked a precise time. Say like one in the afternoon. Maybe twelve-thirty.

I want him here as much as I dread him showing up in the light of day.

Will everything look different in the light?

I turn to Grandma for the fourth time, trying to think of something to talk about. I've been pacing around the house, waiting for him to show.

I'm a bundle of nervous energy. Why am I letting him do this to me?

Why am I doing this to myself?

I'm just so afraid that now he's not going to show and I really want him to show. After all my resistance, after being *so* not interested, I've got it bad.

Damn. This is not how I want to feel right now.

"Honey, sit down. Play on your phone or maybe watch TV. If you don't stop pacing you're going to wear a hole in our carpet."

"I..." Okay, so maybe I am a little antsy.

"Don't worry, Clarissa. I saw the way he looked at you, he will show up soon. That man is not going to just booty call you."

"Grandma!"

"What?"

"You can't..." And now I'm blushing again.

"I'm just saying he will be here, he likes you. He won't stand you up."

I roll my eyes. Booty call, *oh my god*. I can't believe she just said that.

"Clarissa, listen up. You need to be open with him. You can't just wait around the house with me for the rest of your life. You need to get out there again and try to experience the world."

"I'm trying, Grandma."

"Well, you better try harder. That man is your best chance at real happiness."

"How in the world would you know that?" I ask in confusion.

"I know the look he gives you…"

The rumble of his motorcycle coming down our street stops our conversation.

I'm not sure what she means. What look? The look he gives when he is trying to strip me of every single stitch of clothing I have on?

I've known from the time I was in seventh grade, throwing baseballs at opponents, that I was something special.

Your average high school pitcher isn't being scouted for college in tenth grade.

During college, I had scouts for major league teams clamoring for me, the boy with the golden arm. I went through the minors pretty damn quickly out of college.

I didn't have to spend much time in the slums.

Shit. I thought I was hot stuff until I started to notice my velocity and speed starting to drop off. Nothing extreme, but coaches and sports analysts saw it too. I was quickly on my way to becoming a burnout.

Last winter I developed the chip I have on my shoulder now.

I throw at my opponent like he fucked my mom.

I want the guy I'm throwing at to be afraid of me. I want them to be worried. Because I *will* fuck their day up.

I don't stop working out when everyone else does. I

push myself now, I push what I can do. I refuse to allow myself to get into some rut where average is acceptable. I was a phenomenon then and I will be one until I retire.

I won't fizzle out.

The new me has earned a bit of respect in the clubhouse, I think. The guys look to me as a leader.

Missing a couple of games is killing me. I fucking hate it. It's a risk to our record to keep me out of these games, but I respect what they tell me to do.

In the end, I'm still an employee, like everyone else.

I will do what they say but it doesn't mean I won't be heading into the clubhouse and working out with the guys. You can't skip shit like that. If I want to help lead this team to the World Classic and beyond, I need to lead by example.

The call from Jim comes and he tells me the new catcher will be in this morning. I shower and get my ass moving. I ride down to the stadium.

I walk into the locker room and it looks empty until I turn a corner and see a guy in front of Raleigh's old locker. His back is to me as he puts his belongings up, and I don't have any idea of who he is until he turns around at the sound of my footsteps.

Well, fuck me. It's a small world after all.

"Bryce, motherfucking donkey dick, Stevens!" I growl as I grab the guy up in a tight hug.

Hugging him as hard as I can for a moment, I pull back and set the red-faced guy down.

"How the fuck are ya?" I ask.

"Christ, Crass, you trying to break my fucking ribs?" he asks as he rubs his right side.

Bryce Stevens was my roommate back in college, and

my go-to guy as a catcher back then. He was drafted the year ahead of me and spent a while in the minors.

I was pulled up faster but this guy is one of the best catchers around, at least in my opinion.

We've played against each other a few times, but we were in two different divisions so we weren't forced to face each other much.

Bryce is a damn good guy. He is a hard worker and a damn good player on the field. Probably off the field, as well, if what I hear is true.

"Fuck, man, it is good to have you coming in here."

"Thanks, Crass, I'm glad to be here. How's the hand?" he asks as he reaches down and grabs my hand up.

He looks at it from a couple of different angles. The bruises have faded and so has the twitch in my arm.

"Good," I say as I pull it back and check myself. "Guess the rumor mill is going pretty hard on this?"

"Yeah, but not much about what truly happened. It's out there, though, that you and dicksnot had an altercation."

I nod my head, happy that at least all the details aren't out there. I don't want all the team's dirty laundry aired to the world.

Looking at the jersey on the door, I see his name already stitched on, ready to go. "You wanna go toss for a bit?"

"Shit, yeah, but keep the heat down at first. I haven't caught for a heavyweight in a while."

I snicker, he probably hasn't.

Like I said, I have a fucking chip on my shoulder.

It's been some years since I've thrown with Bryce but we fall into an easy rhythm as we go through warming up. Jim steps out to watch and smiles to us. After several fast balls he motions for us both to come over.

"Jackson, Bryce, you guys are looking good. How about throwing a simulated game tomorrow?"

We both nod and I can see the wide smile on Bryce's face. Having Bryce on the team can be nothing but good for us.

"Good. Nine, tomorrow morning, sound good?"

He watches a bit longer as we work out our hand signals and then heads off to be with the rest of the team.

The guys come over to talk to Bryce while we are working out. Bryce has teamed with a couple of them already so his reputation as a solid guy is pretty much taken as a given.

As we are both heading in from the field, he asks, "So what have you been up to this season? I heard you've been making huge changes."

"How about dinner tomorrow night and I talk to you all about it?" I ask as I glance down at my watch.

It's one-thirty and I really want to get over to see Clarissa. I feel down, somewhere in my stomach and balls, I want to see this girl.

Shit, even up in my head I feel the need to see her.

Nodding his head, he watches as I strip down and head straight to the shower. "Damn, man, you in a hurry?"

"Yeah, I need to get out of here quick. I got this girl... Well... I mean we are seeing each other and I want to get over there."

"Like a real date?" he asks with disbelief.

I don't blame him for questioning me on it. He knows the kind of person I have been for far too long.

"Yeah, like a real one."

David, the other catcher, walks past me laughing. "Yeah, I'll believe it when I see it."

They're not wrong about me. Dating and me were two words that haven't been mixed in a long time. If ever.

Shit, neither has responsibility.

This being an adult thing isn't easy as I thought it was when I was younger. The team is looking to me for leadership.

Dating women instead of simply getting my dick wet... What the fuck next? Minivans?

Shaking my head, I dread that thought as I race towards Clarissa's.

The bike rumbles as I make my way through her neighborhood. Some of her neighbors stop to look at me as I pass by but most keep on doing whatever their lives have them doing.

I haven't cruised through the suburbs like this since I left for college. Mom and Dad still live in the small community out in Ohio that they raised me in—even though I've tried to get them to move out here. They like the small town feel.

I'm not sure I could adjust to a small town now that I've been out here for so long.

I like the lights and I like the city sprawl that Los Angeles has. Yeah, there are some pretty damn rough spots but there are some really awesome parts too.

I'm spoiled with where I live, I guess.

Pulling up in front of her house, I shut the bike down

and take a moment to calm myself. No need to go running up to the door like some lovesick fool.

Setting the helmets down, I walk to her door and ring the doorbell.

Clarissa opens the door and her cheeks are flushed with red. "Hello, Jackson, come in."

I smile at her and as I walk by and lean down to kiss her cheek. "What's got you blushing?"

Turning even more red, she pushes me into the living room. "You two need to be nice to me."

I laugh uncertainly, but when I see her Grandmother standing there with a wide smile on her face, I figure I'm not in too much trouble. "How's it going, ma'am?"

"No more of this ma'am stuff, I'm Helen."

"How about you come down to the stadium tomorrow, Helen? It's an off day and we are planning on doing a simulated game with the new catcher."

Her eyes widen and brighten as she says, "I would love to! Will you be driving me down on your motorcycle?"

"Sure. How about I pick you up at 8:30?" I ask.

"That sounds perfect, Jackson, thank you."

I smile at her and nod my head. She's cool as hell and she knows more about baseball than some players I know.

A grumpy sound interrupts our pitching strategy discussion. I look to Clarissa and she is shaking her head. "Are you dating Grandma or me today? I just want to make sure I have my slot in the rotation too..."

Helen laughs, patting me on the arm as she walks towards the kitchen. "There is no way he could handle an older lady like myself."

I eye her as she walks away and laugh. She is probably right.

Clarissa elbows me in the stomach. "Stop checking out my grandma."

Walking out the door, holding hands, she asks, "Do you even own a car?"

"Yeah, but it's jacked. I'm having it looked over to see what my options are. Raleigh busted it up pretty bad."

"Oh... How?"

"Baseball bat. I guess I'm lucky that when he charged me he dropped the bat."

"Yeah, no kidding. So where are we going?"

"Riding down towards the coast and having dinner at a seafood place I like.... then whatever."

She gets to the bike and stands there as I'm strapping my helmet on. Then smiles at me as I strap hers on. I don't think she even notices that it makes her smile when I take care of her.

Getting on the bike, we take off and head out of the city.

The ride home from dinner is nice. The breeze from the ocean and the fading light of the night makes the ride feel like we are one on the bike. We pull off the highway, close to the city, and as I come to a stop at a light I let the purr of the bike die down a bit.

Looking over my shoulder, I say, "I don't want to take you home right now."

She gives me a long hard stare. I can see the gears in

her head spinning as she debates her answer. "Then don't."

I rev the bike up as I turn a quick circle to get back onto the freeway.

My heart is beating as fast as the miles are eaten up by the wheels. I've done a lot of things in my life but I've only ever brought three women back home.

I discovered quickly, back in the days I first moved out here, that it sucks to have a chick stay the night with you.

I mean, seriously, how many times can you tell a chick that she has to get in the cab and go?

That shit gets old.

I've learned since then to keep my conquests at their home or in a hotel somewhere. I like my privacy, and I like knowing a random chick doesn't know where I live.

Driving Clarissa to my home feels different... she's not some random.

Matter of fact, I've never messed around with a chick and not had my balls wet and deep before. Clarissa is different than the others. I want her at my home. I want her with me.

The hills wind us and twist us as we drive past the houses, but once we get to my street I slow us down. I doubt she will remember the route but I'm trying to make it as easy as possible.

Pulling up to the gate of my house, I stop the bike next to the keypad. Leaning over to type the six digit number in, I feel her head turn to the side to give me privacy.

"Hey, you need to watch this. The code is my mom's birthday. Zero-Three-One-Two-Five- Eight."

Shaking her head, she asks, "Why do I need that?"

I pull us up the driveway and loop around the trees in my front yard.

My house is big but the landscaping in the front gives me the secluded look, shielding it from the street. I like privacy and my neighbors are the same way. The trees lining both sides of the property keep us all tucked away and hidden.

I push the button on my key fob to open the garage and pull us in.

Shutting the bike down, I pull my helmet off then lean us to the side. Clarissa climbs off and when she stands there, waiting for me, I can't help but smile at her big gigantic blue eyes. She looks too serious though as I'm taking off her helmet.

"Why do I need to know the code?"

"How else are you supposed to get in if I'm not here? Or if I can't let you in?"

"Who says I'm going to be coming or going that often?"

I smirk. "Me. Unless you want me to chain you to the bedroom? I'm sure I can talk Helen into letting me keep you."

Eyebrows raising, she asks, "What is going on in that big perfect head of yours? You can't just treat me like I'm some slave girl."

"Nah, you will have to submit before I treat you like that."

"You're pushing it."

"Yeah, but you said my head is perfect." Turning away from her I push the button to shut the garage door.

Walking to the door that leads into the kitchen, she reminds me, "I also said it was big!"

"Yeah, but perfect."

We walk into the house and I watch as her mouth falls open at the size of the kitchen.

"Holy cow! My living room is smaller than this!"

Shaking my head, I smirk, "Nah, it's not that big."

We head through the house and her eyes are as big as saucers as she takes in the size of the place. I do a quick tour through the bedroom to show her the deck and the infinity pool that is off the back.

Opening the sliding glass door, I explain, "This is why I bought the house... besides the privacy."

Looking out over the valley, the city is off in the distance. She stands still, taking in the view. "Wow."

Jackson's house is humongous.

It's nearly the size of a mansion, regardless of how much he tries to downplay it. He is obviously proud of it, but not in a bragging sort of way. It's a relief. He may be cocky about most things but at least he isn't cocky about his house or money.

For some reason that settles the uneasiness of him giving me the code to his gate.

I know I shouldn't have let him bring me back here... there's only one place this all will lead to—the bedroom. But the question is should I let it?

Should I give in to him? It would be so easy to just let my defenses to weaken and trust him? Easier than to keep fighting. But will this be just one night of fun? Or is there truly more growing between us?

The view is amazing from here.

I gaze out at the city lights. There is darkness out there trying to blanket the city, but it is held at bay by all those flashing and twinkling lights. I love it, and just soak it in for the longest time, trying to calm the chaos in my head.

Turning away from the city, Jackson fills my view. I didn't realize he was standing so close to me.

Steeling myself, I finally work up the nerve to ask, "Jackson, what exactly is it you are wanting?"

"You. All of you. I want you without any hesitations."

Well, crap.

Looking up into those bright, heated eyes I can feel my stomach dropping. He told me exactly what he wants, and I don't doubt it for a second, but what about the future?

"So you want me just for tonight?" I ask.

Best to get it all out there so there's no confusion or hurt feelings later. At least, that's what I'm telling myself.

"No. I don't think tonight is going to be enough," he says as he moves closer to me.

I take a couple of steps backwards, to put distance between us and my butt pushes up against the railing. A quick glance over my shoulder and I can see there's nothing beyond the railing but a sheer drop.

I can go no further.

I don't know what I expected but I didn't expect this. I didn't expect him to tell me exactly what I want to hear. My heart is thundering and the blood is roaring in my ears.

I wanted to hear those words yet I'm utterly terrified of them.

He puts a hand on either side of me, and I'm trapped.

"I don't do flings Jackson," my voice softly implores him. "I don't do the casual thing."

And I don't do *hurt*.

"I don't want that, Clarissa."

"Then what exactly do you want to come from this?"

He smiles, and he's so close I feel like I'm basking in his warmth. "From what?"

Ugh, he's just not going to make this easy for me, is he? Why does he have to keep pushing me out of my comfort zone. Why must I always be blushing from head to toe when I'm with him?

"You know..." I say lamely.

I am so not going to say it; he knows exactly what my meaning is.

He doesn't respond. No, his smile only seems to grow. As he leans down, *he* only seems to grow.

He kisses my lips.

Gently at first, just brushing his lips across mine. Using the soft, gentle slanting of his mouth over mine as his answer.

Slowly, gradually, he increases the pressure. He's treating me so lightly, so tenderly, I feel like he's doing it intentionally. Maybe he's afraid to spook me? Maybe he knows I'm ready to bolt if he pushes too fast?

I still feel so unsure.

I *know* it will feel amazing, but I also know that afterwards it could hurt like a bitch.

His lips push open, and I feel his tongue lightly trace the contours of my closed lips, urging me to open for him.

I want to. I want to open up, to give in. To take that risk.

I hesitate and he doesn't press. And in that moment of acceptance, I make my decision.

Just do it. Stop being a coward and *live*.

My mind made up, I lean into him, wrapping my arms around his neck and opening my mouth.

There's a moment of surprise, as if he didn't expect it, and then he groans, his tongue pushing past my lips.

I can feel the vibrations of his groan all the way down to my toes.

His hands move from the rail and they encircle me as he lifts me up into his arms. I have never felt so small before. So fragile. So vulnerable in his hands.

He spins around with me, and I wrap my legs around his waist as he carries me into his bedroom. Pressing against him, I can feel his arousal between my thighs and there's an immediate flush of desire flooding my body. He wants me and the knowledge of it only increases my own desire.

Somehow he continues to kiss me as he carries me. His tongue thrusting into my mouth in a rhythm that would trip me up. Reaching his bed, I half expect him to lay me down on it but he lowers me to my feet instead.

I loathe unwrapping my arms from around his neck. I've finally given in and I loathe breaking this connection but there are too many clothes between us. Lips pulling away from mine, my mouth feels tingly and swollen.

There's light in here, coming from a small lamp in the corner, but it's softer, subdued.

My back facing the bed, he moves slowly, purposely as if he has all the time in the world. Hands grabbing my shirt, slowly he lifts it up, pulling it over my head.

I shiver, not because I'm cold, but from self-doubt. What if he doesn't like what he sees? What if he thinks I'm too out of shape? Or too real, not like the models he's used to.

He doesn't stop with my shirt though. He just continues to undress me as if he's eager to see me naked. And I let him. Despite my reservations I want him to get a good view of what I truly am.

If he doesn't like me now, I won't have to worry about this going any further. I won't have to worry about seeing his body and not being able to control myself.

Unclasping my bra, he lets it fall to the floor and freezes as if he's stunned.

"You are stunning, Clarissa," he rasps, and in his bright eyes I feel *beautiful*.

He stares at my breasts like he wants to touch them, wants to taste them but he kneels down and his hands drop to remove my shoes instead. Shoes gone, socks gone, his hands come back up and his fingers quickly and deftly unbutton my jeans. Before my next breath, he's yanking my jeans down and helping me step out of them.

Standing only in my panties, I don't know why, but my hands drop to cover them. Suddenly I'm afraid of losing them. I feel so exposed standing here nearly naked while he's still completely dressed.

"All of you, Clarissa. No holding back," he growls.

He pushes my hands away and I close my eyes. I can't watch this. I can't bear witness.

I feel too exposed.

Thank god I shaved myself and cleaned up down there. I would have died from embarrassment if I hadn't.

Cool air hits me and I feel my panties sliding down my thighs. He sucks in a loud breath and I'm practically buzzing with all my nervous energy. Was that a good breath or does he find me revolting?

"Holy shit!" I screech out as I feel his face push

between my thighs and his tongue come sliding across my clit. "What are you..."

I'm so shocked I just stand here, staring down at the top of his head. Surely, this isn't truly happening? This must be my imagination.

I feel his tongue again and my butt jerks back.

Instinctively, I reach down and try to push his head back. Reaching up, he grabs me by the wrists and then he pushes me. I fall back. With a gasp my back hits the top of the bed and he comes down on top of me.

Once again I try to cover my pussy, but he moves my hands away as his head dives right back between my thighs. I have never felt something like this before. I have never had a man put his mouth where he is putting his. At first it's so stunning and so overwhelming that all I can do is lie here as his tongue traces my outer lips.

"Oh, god," I moan out as his tongue strokes against me again.

He takes a long broad stroke of my pussy, from top to bottom. Leaving me clutching at the blankets and gasping for breath.

Then he presses his tongue hard against my folds and drags it up and up, until he reaches my clit.

He teases me, circling my clit. So close but never quite touching it.

I growl and have the strongest desire to reach down, grab him by the head and force him to lick it. Then suddenly the circling stops and he sucks my clit into his mouth, pulling back a hard suck on it.

The world stops spinning. My mouth opens with a silent scream as I'm overwhelmed with intense, electrifying sensation.

Sucking and flicking, he's caressing yet mashing in a rhythm so complex I burst into a thousand pieces.

It feels like an eternity passes before I float back down from the clouds. He's pulled away from my wet, throbbing sex and the cool air has me shivering all the way down to my toes.

Looking up, I watch him pull his shirt up and over his head, revealing a lot of naked skin. His chest is wide, muscled and hairy, and he kind of reminds me of a lumberjack without his shirt on. I wasn't expecting that but it's so deliciously masculine I like it.

There's not an inch of him that isn't hard, strong, or male.

My eyes move to his hands as they unbutton then unzip his pants, pushing them down his legs. His cock springs forth and inside me something clenches. I've never looked at a cock and *wanted* it before. Large, red, almost angry looking. A part of me is afraid of it, wondering how on earth it's going to fit, and yet another part of me is practically crying in anticipation, telling me this is going to feel so good.

Eyes darting up, he's staring down at my body. His eyes roaming all over me as he drinks me in. He doesn't seem put off by my softness, by all my curves and lack of sharp edges. If anything, his face becomes more intense, there's a new fierceness to him.

He doesn't say it but his eyes are laying claim to me, branding me his.

His eyes are so hot, two blue infernos, yet I'm still cold, hating the distance between us.

Lifting my arms up, I reach for him.

It's almost as if he was waiting for it, waiting for my permission to come down and cover me with his body.

Positioning himself between my thighs, his eyes find mine and lock on.

"All right?" he asks, his voice thick and rough as his fingers brush my hair back.

I nod my head.

My throat is so tight with anticipation, with emotion, I don't think I could speak if I wanted to.

Everything is done slowly, with great deliberation. The way his hairy thighs nudge my quivering thighs open. The way he tenderly strokes my cheek, my hair as he reaches between us.

My eyes dart down, sliding between our bodies, watching. I just have to see this.

Taking himself in his hand, he positions the head of his cock at my entrance.

I'm tight, and I know it. That cock of his is going to split me in two. Maybe if I'm lucky it will cause me to break into a thousand pieces again... That was amazing.

Slowly, he slides the head up and down between my lips. Coating himself with my wetness. I'm so ready for him yet there's still resistance as he pushes forward. I groan and he grunts as he pushes his way in.

There's an unrelenting pressure and a warm, stretching sensation but it doesn't quite hurt yet. He is so big I worry that he won't fit and my hands grip the sheets in a death grip. Then I feel his head slide past the spot of tightness and everything inside of me just gives.

"Oh god, Jackson... Oh god."

"So fucking tight..." he groans out against my neck.

His right arm slides up, under my back and his hand

latches onto my shoulder, holding me there as he pushes further into me. Left hand going to my breast, he grasps it and his rough callouses graze my nipple as he kisses the side of my neck.

Sinking himself to the hilt, I've never felt so full before. So complete.

Is this how I'm supposed to feel? Every fiber of my body, of my very being connected to him?

His body covers mine completely, and he's so warm, so strong, I feel safe. Protected even.

I was so afraid that he would hurt me. That he'd use his charms to get behind the shields I've built and destroy me from the inside out. But looking up into his eyes I know now that fear was foolish. He won't hurt me. He'll do anything but.

The longer I stare up into his eyes, the more and more I fall under his spell. There's such awe, such wonder there I feel like we're discovering something new and magical together.

Slowly, he pulls back and I feel so empty. Then he pushes deep back into me and everything is right in the world again.

He increases the pace, thrusting deeper and harder. His weight sinking me into the mattress as he loses himself.

The bed creaks and the sound of our bodies colliding fills my ears. Back arching, I tip my hips up so I can take more of him, deeper.

"Fuck," he growls, when he bottoms out.

Hands going to his back, my fingers drag down his spine, my nails scoring his skin.

The sensations reaching my brain are almost too

much to withstand. Too much heat, too much friction.

Too much pleasure.

The scratching of my nails only seems to spur him on

I've never felt anything like this before, and perhaps it's because it's so new to me, so intense, but it feels like only seconds later and my body is tensing up.

His cock pounds relentlessly in and out of me.

My world explodes.

Warm waves of pleasure roll through me. I can feel myself clenching down on him, trying to hold him inside me.

His mouth is against mine as he groans, "Fuck, Clarissa, I'm going to come."

Somewhere deep in my brain a light goes off. And while still trapped in the throes of my own orgasm, I realize with sudden clarity that we're not using protection.

Oh, fuck!

My mouth is opening, to tell him to stop. That we're not protected.

But it's already too late.

He swells inside me and then there's an explosion of warmth. And though I know this is bad, very bad, there's something so naughty about it that just knowing he's coming inside me sends me right back over the edge.

I explode with another orgasm. Fireworks burst behind my eyes as my sex contracts and spasms around him.

His head falls forward and he groans and shudders above me as if he's in pain. Vaguely, I'm aware that I'm torturing him but I can't stop what's going on. I can't stop my body from trying to milk from him every last drop.

Coming down together, he kisses me gently on my neck then my cheek. His mouth languidly covers mine, after all of that, and he kisses me deeply.

Pulling back, he stares down into my eyes and says, "God, that was amazing."

I can't hold it in. Sucking in a breath, I tell him, "We didn't use protection!"

"Fuck."

"Fuck," comes out of my mouth before I have a chance to even think about what she said.

Shit. She's right. How the fuck did I forget?

I know the rules; I know that I should always use protection. I've heard the horror stories guys have gone through when it comes to not using it. Shit, I've heard about guys making sure the rubber goes with them when they leave the girl.

Like they take it or flush it.

She pulls her head back at my curse. "I realized right as we came together. It's.... It's okay. It's not the right time of my cycle and I'm on the pill. But we didn't use protection. We were unprotected. I mean... I know I'm clean..."

What the fuck does she think I am, some walking STD?

"No worries from me, I've been tested since my last partner."

Breathing out a sigh of relief, she lays her head back down on the pillow. "Sorry, I didn't..."

Leaning down, I brush my lips across hers again.

Rolling to the side, I lay down on my back, pulling her onto my chest. I hold her tight to me. She moves around a bit before settling her head on my chest. Her fingers run lightly over my abs.

"Wow. That was... amazing. I've never felt like that before."

"You mean you were a virgin?"

Was that what all the hesitation was about? Shit.

She giggles quietly on my chest. "No, not a virgin. I've done it once."

Looking down at her, she looks up into my eyes. "Once?" I ask.

"Yeah, it wasn't a good experience. It hurt pretty badly and as soon as he was done we were done. He told everyone at school about it the next day," she says, and from the sad way she looks I can tell that this is the reason she's been so hesitant and hard to get.

"Some guys are worthless, Clarissa. I'm sorry you had to experience that for your first time."

Twisting her body, she stays on my chest, but is now laying on her stomach. My eyes slide down her body and I feel my cock stirring again. "You really mean that, don't you?"

"Yes. There's no excuse for that shit."

"I forgave him a long time ago; I just haven't forgotten what he did. My grandfather made sure that he didn't mess around with a girl again like that. He was a tough cop."

"Yeah, your grandmother was telling me about him. I got the impression he was one of the good guys."

"He was."

Inwardly, all this talk about good guys and bad guys is making me wince. I know I'm not one of the good ones, but I'm not entirely bad. I know this is corny as fuck, but being with her just makes me want to be a better man.

We lay there looking at each other, just staring into the others eyes. Hers have only grown more beautiful, and they're far too knowing, far too penetrating. She is gazing into my soul right now as if I've laid it completely bare for her.

"Is this still more than just a one night thing?" she asks softly.

"Yes, for me it is." I answer honestly, and it is.

Tonight wasn't enough. Not nearly enough.

Maybe it never will be.

I know that what we did tonight was the best sex I have ever had, hands down. And I have never been with someone who has felt so right.

"Okay, I'm trusting you to not hurt me, Jackson. If you do I promise you won't get another chance."

"I won't."

"Good," she grins up at me.

That fucking grin has so much promise in it. I can see a glint in her eyes as her hand slides down to my cock. It was flagging for a while, semi-hard, waiting to know if we could play again.

Gripping my cock in her hand, she says, "I have always wanted to try it like this."

Crawling up my waist, she straddles my hips as she lifts up. Her breasts look so inviting I lean up and capture one of her swollen nipples in my mouth. I suck lightly on it as she slides my throbbing head between her lips and then she's lowering herself down on it.

Slowly impaling herself on my cock, her pussy walls clench down tightly on each inch that pushes inside of her.

It feels so fucking amazing.

I wasn't kidding when I said how absolutely perfect we feel together. Filling her completely, it was as if she was *made* to have me inside of her.

She rolls her hips back and forth, then rises up. I can feel each inch sliding out of her, the cold air hitting my wet shaft that has been buried deep inside her molten walls.

She falls back down.

"Oh god!" she moans as she rises up then down again.

Latching my mouth on her nipple, I let my teeth lightly graze her tender flesh before sucking down hard on it. She grunts with another drop and then pulls my head tight to her chest.

"That's it, Jackson, please keep doing that."

My tongue swipes around her nipple as I suck. My hands grip her ass, helping her lift herself up. As she comes back down I thrust up as hard as I can inside her.

Her breathing stops for a long moment then she shrieks out in ecstasy, "Fuck!"

The walls of her pussy are clenching so tightly around my cock, I fight my way up, battling the tight walls that try to hold me still.

"Fuck, Clarissa, I'm going to come so soon."

"In me. In me! Fill me, please," she moans and writhes, still trapped in her throes.

I try to hold out longer but it's fucking impossible. She's so tight, so wet, so fucking beautiful, I can't hold back.

She's mine.

Mine, dammit. And I want to fill her until she overflows.

Thrusting up inside of her, I feel each and every hot jet of cum spilling into her. She continues to clench down on me as I moan around her nipple.

She locks up on me again as I slowly finish.

Falling down onto my chest, she rests her small body there as she nuzzles into my neck.

Still catching our breath, she peeks up at me from beneath her hair and asks in soft wonder, "Is it always so good?"

I think about that for a moment then say, "Only with you."

Sometime during the night, I feel Clarissa slide away from where she was snuggled up against me in bed. I watch in the moonlight that filters through the window as she goes to her pants on the floor and gets her phone from a pocket. She walks to the bathroom and I can hear her make a quiet phone call.

When she comes back to bed, I move the blankets for her as she snuggles back in. Her small body wraps around me.

"Everything okay?" I ask.

"Yeah, I just wanted to make sure grandma knew where I was and to not wait for me."

"Will she be okay?"

She laughs quietly. "I asked the same thing and she

made a rather risqué comment about us. So yeah, I think she is happy and will be more than fine."

"Do I want to know?"

"Probably not..."

We lay there for a moment until she asks, "Have you ever heard of doggy style?"

Her hand drifts down to my waist.

My cock is so hard and throbbing that I'm not sure which happened first. Her hand touching it or the words going through my head.

The morning comes too early, but thankfully my alarm woke us with just enough time for us to grab a shower together. It was a very long, very steamy shower, though, so as we're leaving the house she calls her grandmother —letting her know we are on the way and to be ready.

The drive over is quicker now for some reason. Maybe it's because I don't want to be separated from her, and I'm all too aware of every minute we have.

But she will be with me today, and her grandmother, so it won't be a bad day.

And I get to start throwing again. Just the thought of it makes me happy as a motherfucker.

After pulling up to her grandmother's house, I take my time unstrapping her helmet and give her one last, deep kiss before I let her walk away from me.

Her grandmother smiles to us both as we walk in and comes up to hug us.

"Goodness, Clarissa, are you okay? You're limping a bit."

Clarissa starts to blush as she says, "Oh yes... fine... Just not use to riding the bike so much."

Her grandmother looks to me with a grin and says, "Well, I sure hope I don't limp like you do when I'm done with it."

"Grandma!" Clarissa shrieks and hides her face in her hands in mortification.

I'm not sure who is laughing harder though, me or the old woman who just became my best friend.

Clarissa disappears into her room and we're still snickering when she comes back out wearing fresh clothing.

Looking between the both of us, she frowns like a scolding mother. "You two are incorrigible."

After locking up the house, Clarissa jumps into her car and I help her grandmother climb onto the back of my bike.

Strapping her helmet on securely, Helen smiles at my help. "This is so exciting, Jackson!"

"You better be safe with my grandmother, Jackson!" Clarissa yells out her car window before we back out of the driveway and head over to the ball field.

I so cannot believe Grandma would say something so... brazen like she did with Jackson. But then again it shouldn't surprise me... she was like that with grandpa too. Loved to say brassy things then give him a kiss on his cheek whenever he got embarrassed.

I think it's her way of showing she's no pearl-clutching, easily offended old woman. She's only sixty-three, I have to remind myself every time she says something like that.

She is far more with the times than I ever give her credit for.

Sometimes I forget she and grandpa were still young when they took me on as their responsibility. Not that they would ever call me that, but when mom and dad died they took me on as if I was a child of their own.

She would have been forty-three and he was forty-six. Hardly past their child bearing years. They married young and had a child nine-months later. I was with them by the time I was one year old. They're all I've ever known. How hard it must have been for them to lose their daughter, my mother, and then taking me on.

They never complained about me, least not that I ever heard or felt. No, they loved me with everything they had in them.

Thanks to them, I am who I am.

I pull up to the gated area where a guard is standing next to his booth, speaking with Jackson. He waves us through then smiles at me as I pass. We drive through the parking lot located right next to the stadium, parking in a section labeled guest parking.

He has a small backpack he keeps attached to the bike slung over his shoulder as he helps grandma off the bike.

She is all smiles as she climbs down, her eyes bright as she says, "I forgot how good it feels to ride on a bike like that. Feels like flying."

Nodding my head, I step up to her side and we walk through the player's entrance together. Her eyes are so wide and so bright, and her smile hasn't faltered yet. I know she's getting way more out of this than I am and I can't help but look at Jackson, feeling intense gratitude towards him for doing this.

Jackson ushers us into the lobby and points to the waiting area. "If you guys could wait here, I will be right back."

As soon as we are alone, Grandma asks, "How was your night last night?"

Blushing, I say, "It was... fine. Everything go okay at the house?"

"Yep, I just had a meal in front of the TV, watching the sports channel. It was a pretty good night for me."

No doubt she loved it, she is a sports addict.

We talk quietly for a few minutes before Jackson appears out of the hallway he disappeared down. He's changed into his practice clothing and looks even taller with his cleats on.

Holy crap, I'm having a hot flash. Decked out in his uniform he is even more handsome. There's just something about a guy in a uniform that's sexy as hell.

Though there's a frown on his face, and his mood has completely changed.

"Is everything okay, Jackson?" I ask.

"Yeah, Clarissa, just got some news about a player being picked up."

Grandma must understand what's going on, she makes a disgusted huff. "Well, that was quick."

"Yeah, disgustingly so," Jackson agrees.

I'm not really sure what's going on until Grandma mutters a dirty word about Raleigh.

Oh.

"But why?" I ask.

"Because he's a good player, and the team that picked him up doesn't mind people of his... caliber on their team." Shaking his head, he goes on. "That and they are looking to be one of the teams we will face in the post-season race to the Championship."

He stands there for a long moment in thought, and to me it's obvious how upset he is but he seems to be trying to internalize it. He looks both angry and determined.

Shaking his head and snapping himself out of his thoughts, he smiles at me for a long moment before saying, "You guys are not properly dressed."

Turning around, he calls over his shoulder. "Be right back."

He jogs down the hallway and disappears again. A couple of minutes later and he is back with two baseball jerseys. He escorts us to a bathroom to change.

"Is this... a real one?" Grandma asks, and I swear she is about to swoon.

Nodding his head, he says, "Yep, two of mine."

Walking into the bathroom, I can't help but grin. He is so trying to lay his claim on us. The shirts are huge on us but Grandma and I couldn't be happier.

After checking ourselves in the mirror, we head back out and he smiles at both of us. "Ready to go?"

We walk back the way he came and he leads us through a series of hallways. "If you guys want, you can hang out closer to the action today. You don't want to sit in the stands, do you?"

I think about it for a moment but I don't know where else we would sit.

"Not if we don't have to," Grandma chimes in, and I swear her grin is getting even bigger.

I guess I'll just have to trust her on this.

We turn down a long hallway, and it's a bit of a walk but then suddenly we are in the dugout for the team.

There are other men in the dugout already and each smiles or touches their hat to us in greeting.

Names are exchanged and Grandma is so excited she is practically buzzing with happiness. I haven't seen her like this in a long time... She is genuinely a happy person, but now? She's glowing.

Jackson leads us over to one guy in particular, outfitted in catchers gear. "Clarissa, Helen... This is Bryce

Stevens. A new catcher for the Stars and an old friend of mine."

Grandma pumps his hand enthusiastically and exclaims excitedly, "We are so going all the way!"

Everyone looks at her for a moment and jaws hit the floor. I'm sure mine too is on the floor.

Has she had a seizure? Did she just have an attack, dementia setting in?

Realizing what she just said, she quickly explains, "To win the Championship!"

***

Watching Jackson on the mound, my thoughts keep swirling around in my head. He is a different person up there. Gone are the light and teasing smiles. He looks angry, angry at the world and ready to prove it.

I overhear a couple of guys who look like coaches off to the side, talking about what he does. Talking about how hard he is throwing, that his velocity is amazing. Words that sound like they should be attached to a scientific paper come out of their mouths. Velocity, angle of deceleration, and rate of drop off. I have no clue what any of it means but they seem to be pleased, and everyone else as well.

I can't tell though; all I can see is his face. It's almost scary how intense he looks, scary and so very arousing. I shouldn't be squirming in the dugout seats like I am, afraid that I'm ruining my panties but I am.

Grandma has looked over at me a couple of times, asking me if I'm okay. I swear she knows what's going through my head and is torturing me.

Finally, they finish up with the simulated game. They used Jackson, a catcher, and a couple of guys to field the balls. Jackson threw about sixty or so pitches until everyone was satisfied with his performance. He is like a god up there. Tall, dark and so fierce, but now he's smiling broadly.

Grandma and I follow along as the coaches talk to Jackson and his friend. Before he heads into the locker room to change, he smiles and leads us to the waiting room.

This could be my life, I think as I wait with Grandma. I could be with a man who competes for a living as a professional baseball player. I know if I did it would come with a ton of headaches...

Like could I honestly deal with him being on the road all the time?

What would I do while he was gone? What if we have children? Can they be without a father all the time?

That worry is the scariest of them all. I may not have had traditional parents but I did have my grandparents.

Would I be more like a single mother? What if he gets traded? Would I have to move away from Grandma?

Shit, my mind is so not ready for all these thoughts, and I know I'm getting ahead of myself.

We only made love once... he wants more, I know that, but what's more? What am I getting myself into here?

Shaking my head, I stand up when he returns from the locker room freshly, showered.

There's a huge grin on his face as he asks, "So, what did ya think?"

"I'm scared for whoever you throw at next. You looked really mad," I answer honestly.

"Nah, I just have to get into my zone."

"That's some zone," Grandma says as we walk out to the parking lot. I stop at the car as Jackson stands in front of me.

Leaning down, he kisses me on the forehead then my lips. And it's so tender, so sweet, I'm having flashbacks of last night and for a moment I forget where I am. I reach my arms around his neck and kiss him right back. Whatever thoughts I had in my head from earlier fly away in the heat of the moment.

Pulling back from me, he says, "I'll see you tonight, babe. Have a good shift."

Grandma winks at me as they get back on the bike. He starts it up with a roar and I follow them out of the parking lot. He goes one way and I take the other, and I don't like it.

I feel somewhere deep down I should be following him wherever he goes.

The snap of my arm as I threw the ball today was satisfying. I don't like taking a break like we did with the pitching rotation. I need to be there ensuring that we don't lose our place in the standings.

Finding and claiming Clarissa as my own though is a bright spot. She's mine now, and I wasn't kidding when I said I would chain her to my house if I could.

Then again I might just bring her with me if she is willing.

Being on the road is going to be tough on us, though I figure we'll make it work regardless. We just need to figure out what to do.

Last night was exactly what we needed. No more games, no more refusing what is obvious. We belong to each other. No one else will satisfy me like she did, and I'm not going to bother worrying about it.

She is the one my body craves.

Dropping off Clarissa's grandmother leaves me with time on my hands. No time like the present, I guess, to ruin my good mood. I turn the bike back onto the main roads and drive over to the mechanic who is looking over my car.

The car is going to be okay, he reassures me, but fuck that. I can still see the dents and shattered glass in my head.

The fucker Raleigh hurt my hand and fucked up my car.

I'm standing there for a long moment as the mechanic watches me stare at the vehicle. It was brand fucking new. Not a single scratch or ding in the black paint.

Now it's a turd. Fuck this shit.

"You able to tow this over to a car lot?"

His eyes widen at me. "You gonna trade this in over some dents and shattered glass?"

"Yeah."

Dents, shattered glass and the thought of Raleigh fucking my ride over. The knowledge that every time I get into this vehicle I know it's been fucked up by him just rankles my nerves.

"Okay... Where you want me to tow it?"

Shrugging my shoulders, I honestly don't know. I would buy another but that doesn't feel right. I want something new and something fucking fast.

Fuck the Lexus, I need something better.

"Not sure, I'll call you."

"Alright man," he says.

I'm betting he thinks I'm crazy, but this feels right.

Straddling the bike, I hit the starter. The roar feels good under my body. I want to get away from this place. The fucking car sitting there feels like a ghost at my back.

Revving the bike up, I head towards the part of this city I don't frequent often. Beverly Hills. Home of the obscenely rich and the wish they could be rich.

I'm not dressed for car shopping in this part of town but fuck it, I need a car and I want it right now. I've made my mind up on that.

I drive up and down the streets as I look at car lot after car lot.

Rolls Royce has a nice ring to it, but I don't think I'm quite the right fit for one of their cars. McLaren and Ferrari... Nah, they aren't my style. Audi and BMW are okay, but not right either.

I drive around for a while longer. I've looked at most of the lots and so far, nothing has caught my eye.

Stopping at a burrito place, I sit outside to people watch and car watch. A lot of people walk by while I sit there and so do cars. Nothing, though, that grabs at me.

I want something that pulls me to it, like Clarissa did... I don't give a shit if other people like it. I just want to be happy.

Hopping back on the bike, I try one more circuit around the area to see if I see anything.

I shouldn't compare my search for a car with my relationship with Clarissa. I shouldn't, but in my own head who the fuck cares if I do. Not me, I guess, as I think of how I knew right away looking at my short sexy woman that she was it for me. I want that with my car, one look and I'm hooked.

Driving around in circles sucks. I head down a couple last streets before I turn around towards home. Today I guess I'm striking out.

I head down a small street and almost cause a pile up behind me as I suddenly slow.

There, right in the fucking window, is what I want.

Swinging back around to drive on the lot, I pull into a vacant parking spot. The sign over the door reads Aston Martin. Never tried one of these cars, but the one in the window has me entranced.

I walk into the building, staring at the beautifully sculpted red car. Walking around the vehicle, I check out every inch of her. She is sleek, shiny and looks like she is meant to fly. Staring at the back of the vehicle, I see the model of the car is called Vanquish.

"What do you think?" An older gentleman asks me as I finally turn away from the car.

I grin, "I want it."

Laughing loudly, he says, "Let's go for a drive."

Leading me out of the building, he walks with me as we head over to a black model of the same car I was just looking at.

"I want the red one," I say, sounding almost childish to my own ears.

"Okay, but let's drive a test model of it first. I want you to see what it feels like."

Nodding my head, I slip myself into the vehicle and feel how it molds to me like a glove. Inspecting the trim and interior as the man gets in the passenger side, my grin only grows. It's as sexy on the inside as it is on outside, just like my girl.

Handing over the keys, he asks, "So, you ready to fall in love?"

I nod my head. "Already did. Now I gotta see how she feels about it."

Pulling out of the lot, we head out of the city and back towards the hills, where there is less traffic and more importantly less cops.

Twisting and turning up the hills, I put the car through her paces, making sure she can handle what I want. I smile, she certainly can. The engine does everything I ask of it and I can feel there still a large unused portion of it just waiting to be unleashed.

When we return to the lot, I walk right up to the red Vanquish and nod my head. "Let's do the paperwork."

There's a pause before the salesman says, "Two-eighty."

I suppose he's gotta.

Staring at the car, I don't even bother pretending to think about it. "Done."

Pulling my cellphone out of my pocket, I dial up my accountant, "Jackson! How are you doing?"

"Great, Jeremy, just great. Look, I need you to get some money moved around. I want to buy a car."

"Okay, let me see... wait, didn't you just buy one five months ago?" he asks me with a bit of hesitation.

This is why he's my accountant—he's just like my agent, looking out for me and not his own paycheck. He knows if I go broke spending money like an asshole I will not be able to pay him. So he gets a little selfish with my money.

"Yeah, it's a loss. It's been beat up pretty bad in a base-ball-bat-meets-car kind of way."

"Uh..." he mutters as he waits for me to go on.

"I need you to arrange for it to be sold or trashed, whatever we need to do. I'm done with it. Shit, you can get it repaired and keep it as a Christmas gift, or donate it to one of those vocational schools. Kids need to learn how to repair stuff right?"

"*Jesus*, Jackson. What the heck are you buying?"

"An Aston Martin Vanquish."

"Oh... Well..."

"I can cover that cost right?" I ask.

"Of course, you could buy quite a few with how much money you have."

"So can we get going on the *buying it right now* thing?

"Okay, where is it at?"

Giving him the address, I say, "Now I need two-eighty plus whatever fees and taxes. I want the car today, Jeremy. Like I want to drive home right now."

Sitting down in the office, I let Jeremy talk with the older guy who went on the ride with me. Turns out his name is Gus and he is quite used to having buyers getting what they want right away. He promises to have my bike dropped at my house, so I'm more than happy to get the fuck out of there with my new baby.

I try not to squeal tires as I leave the lot, but fuck it. This bitch is mine now.

That's exactly what this car is, a bitch and she is all mine. She is fast, strong and just begging to be put through her paces. Fuck, I need to see if I can reserve some time at a track somewhere. I want to see what she can do.

I whip around a hairpin turn on my way home and love how she stays right the fuck there on the ground with me as we accelerate.

My mind finally sated from buying a new car, it slips back to Clarissa. She's mine now. Last night cemented that. There is no doubt in my mind about that, we are what each other need. No matter what, I want her with me.

Pulling in front of my house, I sit there, staring at the front door. I could go in and sit around for a while but that doesn't appeal to me. I need something else. I need to see Clarissa again.

She's like some kind of drug, I need another dose of her.

I drive right back the way I came, not bothering to slow my speed down as I come out of the hills.

Pulling in front of the busy diner, I step out of the vehicle and key the alarm fob. She's locked up nice and tight. Maybe I should see if I can get an alarm for Clarissa too. That way both of my girls are secure if I'm not around.

Walking into the restaurant, I wave to Clair and she smiles at me from behind the counter. I head to an empty booth and wait for her to get free.

Browsing through my phone, I scan over the sports news and frown at the headlines. They are still talking about Raleigh and me, but now they are going over the odds of our teams making it to the Championship against each other. Fuck, that would be something.

I doubt it will happen though, too much happens in the postseason games before the Championship, but it would be something.

Turning from my phone, I watch as Clarissa buses two tables and fills coffee for another. She is a little whirlwind of activity as she works. I don't think she ever takes a breath of air.

She appears at my table with my food, gives me a quick kiss on my cheek and then she is gone again.

I eat all the food as I watch her and the more I see of her, the hungrier I get. My mouth is practically watering as I stare at her bending over. I don't give a fuck what people say about the tacky pants most waitresses have to wear, she makes them look way too good.

When she finally gets a breather, she comes over to me. Sitting down across from me, she leans back and blows a slow breath out.

Brow creasing, she asks, "Why are you looking at me like that?"

"Like what?"

"Like you want to eat me."

"Because I do. Right now, if I could find a way..."

She frowns and looks at me like she thinks I'm crazy. "I have been working all day. I'm sweaty and dirty. I am sooo gross right now."

Shrugging my shoulders, I couldn't give a fuck. "Doesn't change what I want to do."

"You are so weird," she says, laughing.

I can only nod.

"So what have you been doing today?" she asks, leaning forward and grabbing my hand across the table.

Nodding my head out the window, I point at the red car in the parking lot. "I got me a new girl."

Her eyes widen as she says, "Holy crap! What is that?"

"A Vanquish."

"Wow."

Wow, it's been three weeks, almost four, and I've become so hooked on seeing Jackson that I can barely stand the time he is away from me.

I have filled my vacant time here and there with work and trying to get ready for heading back to school. Those things don't take enough time though.

I find myself pacing around the living room during Jackson's games. As soon as we figured out we couldn't see all of his games because of the different cities and their broadcast priorities, we ordered a baseball package from our cable company.

Watching him throw during games is different now than when I used to watch with Grandma. Now I'm not just a rabid fan of the Stars, but dating their top pitcher.

Should I even bother to fight the feelings of arousal I get when I watch him go out there and stomp around the pitcher's mound? He does it on purpose, I know it. When I asked why he looked so mad out there he explained it's because he wants to scare the batters—make them think he hates them.

Stomping and scaring them is just how he does it.

He's also admitted that sometimes he throws a lot closer to the batter than necessary if he wanted to send a message. Crap, the first time he did that I thought it was on accident until the next time he came up to bat the pitcher did the same thing.

Grandma had to calm me down from screaming my head off at the pitcher. The women and men around us were laughing at me. I couldn't help it though. I don't like someone trying to hurt my guy.

That's another thing. Grandma and I are not expected at the park when Jackson pitches, but the tickets are always waiting for us whether we show or not. Most games I'm able to trade off with another server.

Though when I can't, Grandma still goes to watch. Heck, she now goes to all the games that she can. She loves it.

The people around our seats have adopted grandma and me in, especially since we are sitting in the *wive's* section.

I nearly had a heart attack when one woman welcomed me to it.

She's the wife of the right fielder, Marcy. When she told us where we were sitting I quickly tried to explain I wasn't a wife. Turns out most aren't either. It's a mixture of parents, wives and serious girlfriends.

Sitting there is really cool though. The seats are amazing and right behind the home team dugout. Most of the time the section is at least half full, and as of late, completely full.

It's almost the end of the season. The Stars have secured their playoff spot in the tournament for the Championship. There is an electric current in the air as people are abuzz with excitement.

This is our year. We are going to take the Championship, no second place for us.

I've never been much of a fan of sports until now. Now I'm constantly trying to learn about baseball and all the small little details that go with it. Jackson is more than happy to help with teaching me things, but even he has to shut me off from asking questions after a while.

I apparently *harass* him.

That's a lie, he loves it.

But seriously, I text him all the time with questions. I don't know what has come over me, but it's like I have become a sponge. I want to know everything I can about his world. I want to be a part of it as much as I can.

My phone chirps loudly, it's a text from Jackson. He's been out of town for eight days and it has all but killed me.

I don't like this at all. This is the longest he has been gone so far and it sucks. I want his body next to mine. I need his heat and presence.

Jackson: Sleeping?

Rolling around in my sheets, they're messed up around me. The bed is comfortable enough, but it doesn't have him in it. This sucks. I can barely sleep a night if he isn't here. The only time I sleep is if I'm exhausted from work.

Me: Of course not. You've been gone too long.

I check the clock, it's only eleven-thirty but it feels so much later.

Tonight was an off night from work and I have done nothing but hang out here at the house. Jackson was on a travel home day so he must have just got in.

Jackson: Come to your front door.

My heart skips a beat as I hurry to dress in a pair of jeans and a t-shirt. Pulling my hair back into a ponytail, I slip a Stars baseball cap on.

Hurrying out to the living room, I say to Grandma, "He's back!"

Swinging the door open wide, I see him standing there on my porch, smiling widely at me.

Yelping, I jump up into his arms, wrapping my legs around his waist. Kissing him hard on the mouth, I feel his scruffy beard against my face. He smells so good, like a man should smell.

My tongue slides into his mouth easily as he holds me tight to his chest.

After a long time, we pull apart and I start to blush as I peek over my shoulder. Grandma is laughing at us.

Sitting me back down, he asks, "Mind if I come in?"

Nodding my head, I drag him into the house by the hand. He looks tired. Tired, but very happy when I smile at him.

"How was your flight?" I ask.

"Not bad. A delay in Denver, so longer than planned but nothing too bad." He stretches up his arms as he rocks his hips. I hear some popping throughout his body as he does it again.

Looking down into my eyes, I feel pierced by his baby blue depths. He holds my eyes as he asks Grandma, "Mind if I steal her for the night? Tomorrow is an off day and I have plans for her."

I can see her smile out of the corner of my eye and she waves her hand. "Have a goodnight you two."

I all but yank him out the front door as we head to his red car. Holy crap it is a beautiful car. If I didn't know how much he cares for me, I would think he was having an affair with her. He loves it that much.

Stopping in the middle of the yard, he pulls the keys from his pocket and hands them to me. "Can you drive? I'm exhausted."

Grinning widely, I nod my head. I snatch the keys from his hands and head over to the driver's side. Getting in, I press the button on the side of the seat that automatically conforms the seat to my height and adjusts the mirrors for me.

I was shocked the day after he bought the car. He had me in it, driving us around—just like that.

He is so....more awesome that I could ever imagine. He shares any and everything with me. He tells me all the time what's his is mine. He offers me his house and his heart... and if I wasn't already falling for him I would be worried. But I'm falling for him. Oh my god, how I am.

Should I be falling in love with someone so quickly? I have no clue. It's not like I have much life experience with such things. I am though... and I'm not sure what to do about it.

Reaching his house, we enter through the garage. I can tell he's exhausted. On the drive over his eyes were closed more often than they were open.

Pulling him into the bedroom, I strip him down to his boxers, and then push him into bed. I climb in after him and curl up against his muscular chest.

He is asleep in seconds.

If I wasn't just as tired, I'd be a little worried about him not ravishing me...

But eight days is a long time to be unable to sleep through the night without searching for the other part of your heart.

Sometime in the middle of the night I wake to find myself grinding up against Jackson's thigh. Wet and throbbing to the core, my fingers slowly traced the contours of his stomach muscles. Each time I touch certain spots I can sense Jackson waking more and more.

I know he's exhausted but he's had a couple of hours of sleep now, and I just can't seem to help myself...

His beautiful cock, which was lying dormant against his thigh, quickly rises. His breath stills, ending its deep and sleepy rhythm.

Exhaling loudly, he grabs my hand, pushing it down to his cock. I use his own precum to wet my hand and pump my fist along his velvety shaft.

He groans, "Clarissa," and grabs me by the hips. Lifting me up, he helps me straddle him.

Finally, I get to do what I've been dreaming about doing for eight long days. With his help, I lower myself down, impaling myself on his slick, thick cock.

He's so big and I'm so needy, he stretches me until I feel like I'm going to burst.

"Jackson," I groan as I bottom out. I can take no more of him but I know he has more to give.

"Fuck," he growls. "I've missed you."

Inside, I clench, feeling a jolt of emotion and sensation with the knowledge.

He groans again and his fingers dig into my hips.

"I missed you too," I say, my voice barely above a whisper in the darkness. "I hate being away from you," I admit.

He sucks in a sharp breath. Fingers squeezing me, he helps me lift up and then I drop down, slamming onto his cock.

"Me too, baby. Me too," he grunts.

And then there are no more words, just sensations.

With Jackson's help, I bounce on top of him until I reach my climax.

But as I freeze up, my muscles locking and my pussy spasming, he pushes me over and proceeds to fuck me like a madman.

It's been so long and we're both so desperate. We're frantic with our need for each other, frantic to re-establish this connection.

The waves of pleasure and bliss seem to last for an eternity, yet I know we've only been at it for minutes.

He lets out one last long groan and I feel him twitch and swell inside me. His weight falls upon me. Yet again I feel warm and sticky.

We didn't use protection.

Sated. Exhaustion creeps back in. He rolls over, pulling me with him, and I snuggle back up to his chest.

His hand strokes through my hair and though our hunger for each other has been satisfied for the moment, as I drift back to sleep I feel something much bigger hanging between us, left unsaid.

We're driving to some secret destination, and just the memories of last night have me rubbing my legs together in anticipation. I can't wait to get him back in bed and have my way with him again.

Looking over, I watch his face. He is so handsome when he is focused on doing something. Like when he's on the mound, pitching, or like right now, driving. His eyes get sharp with focus and his jaw is set. He looks intense.

I tried to pry our secret destination out of him but nothing worked. Not even using a blowjob as an incentive. But then again he probably knows he'll get it later anyway, if he wants it.

He's steadfast and set on doing this. Whatever this is.

My hand slides up and down his thigh on its own accord.

He growls but keeps driving. "Clarissa, you are going to get us in trouble if you don't stop."

"Stop what?" I ask in a low throaty voice. I'm doing it intentionally because I love to watch his body physically start to react. He loves to hear me get all throaty and sexy for him.

Lifting my hand from his thigh, he puts it back in my lap. "Be a good girl. I don't think you want me to pull over to the side of the road and fuck you silly."

"Don't be so sure!" I say, and I'm kinda serious.

I have no clue what has come over me these past few weeks, but I'm absolutely crazy for him. I'm always craving him. His touch, his smell.

Being filled by him.

Oh my god, I'm such a pervert now. Everything is becoming sexual with me.

He grins at me, and gives me a heated look. I shiver as his gaze roams pointedly over my thighs and breasts before he's staring hard through the windshield again.

I guess he's giving me a taste of my own medicine.

"We will be there soon, please be patient."

"Where are we going?" I ask. "We are in the middle of nowhere."

I don't recognize anything about the area. All around us is just grass and trees, and land that looks like it's been cleared for farming. With how long we've been driving we could be anywhere by now.

Looking down to my phone, I shoot a text off to Grandma asking her about how her night was. Thankfully, talking to her helps pass the time. Right now it's either keep trying to get Jackson to pull over and fuck me silly or go crazy trying to figure out our destination and the meaning of it.

Slowing down, Jackson turns down a back road and when I look up from my phone my mind goes blank with shock.

"You brought me to a horse ranch?" I ask in disbelief.

"Yep."

"And *why*?"

He so should have discussed this with me first.

"You're going to teach me to ride. I talked to your grandmother and we both thought this would be good for you."

"You what? What do you mean you talked to my grandma about me?"

"We talk or text all the time, babe." He smiles at me as he parks the car in a small lot.

I'm not sure how I feel about that. It definitely feels like I'm being ganged up on.

"You do?"

"Well yeah, she's really cool to talk to. Anyways, like I told you before, she likes me more than you."

I roll my eyes and feel my lips wanting to curve into a smirk. "No, she doesn't. I already asked her."

"She has to say that to you, you're her blood."

God, he really is full of himself.

Groaning, I look around, checking out what I can see of the area. This is so not what I thought our day would be.

Spotting the horses in the field, I stare long and hard at them. I can almost feel how good it was to ride. "Why are we really here, Jackson?"

"Because neither your grandmother nor I could figure out why you stopped riding and we think it's a shame that you did."

"It's not..." I press my lips together and snort out my breath. I don't think he's doing this to be malicious, but it is very heavy-handed. "Look, can we go home?"

"No. Not until you at least tell me why."

Ugh and crap. This is not a conversation I want to have, especially right now.

"Look, it was just stupid stuff that I let get to me."

"What kind of stuff?" he presses as he reaches over and takes hold of my hand.

"Teenage stuff." I want to cross my arms across my chest but I don't. Shit, I still feel like a kid talking about this stuff.

"Tell me," he implores. "I have all day and absolutely no reason to judge you."

I flick my eyes to his face and stare at him long and hard.

At first he gives me that intense look, like I'm a batter at the plate he's staring down. Then his eyes soften as he feels me retreating, and they plead with me. He seriously wants to know.

Taking a long moment, I suck in a breath and slowly breathe it out, avoiding the inevitable. I feel so foolish talking about this stuff, but I know he is serious. He won't let this drop until I tell him everything.

"Remember what I told you about me losing my virginity?"

"Yes."

"Well, it was well known that I was a horse riding nut. Like competitions and vacations... I would spend days on days telling everyone about riding and about the horse my grandfather bought me."

"You own a horse," his eyebrows raising, "I wonder why your grandmother didn't tell me that..."

"No ,we sold her about a year before Grandpa died."

"Oh."

"Well, back then it became known I was pretty good at it and had won medals."

"So... Why would you stop?"

"Well... I think I lost my hymen at some point while riding. When Robbie took my virginity he was a bit shocked there wasn't any blood but kept going anyways. Afterwards... he told people about it and in their eyes I wasn't a virgin. And since he knew my love of horses, he threw some innuendo in the mix."

Shaking my head, I frown. "Nothing nasty but I was the horse girl who must have fucked a lot, and they started making fun of my horse riding. It got pretty bad actually. I never told Grandma or Grandpa because what could they do? Nothing. They would only end up embarrassing me more about it."

"One of the boys said the reason why I liked horses so much was because they were the only things big enough I could feel between my legs. It pushed me away from riding. I know I shouldn't have let it, but I did."

I want to shrug my shoulders and act as if it all didn't still bother me, but it does. After all these years it still hurts.

"Well, fuck them," Jackson says as he squeezes my hand.

He opens his door and gets out. Walking over to my side, he opens my door and extends his hand. Helping me out, he pulls me into a tight hug.

I don't know how long we stand here, just hugging, but I can feel myself pulling strength from him.

"Those kids were jackasses," he murmurs into my hair and kisses the top of my head. "Don't you think it's time to start moving on, Clarissa?"

I think about it for a long moment. It feels like the question is loaded, like there's more than one meaning to it. Time to start moving on from the past, time to start making new memories with him?

Nodding my head, I agree. I want to get over this shit. It's been long enough that the pain is just a faded memory.

In fact, I feel pretty fucking stupid for letting those

assholes take something away from me that meant so much.

But still, a part of me is afraid to do this. Afraid that I've let so much time pass that I can't. I cling to Jackson's hand as he leads us up to a barn with a large house not far from it.

I don't know if he's doing it intentionally, but he feels like a rock. Solid and full of purpose. A living, breathing well of strength I can draw from.

Raising his voice, he calls out, "Hello?" And squeezes my hand.

A woman steps out of a stall, wiping her brow. "Hello to you! Are you Jackson and Clarissa?"

"Yes, ma'am, we are," Jackson flashes a grin and instantly I feel myself lightening with his enthusiasm. Looking between the two of them I feel myself relaxing. This is a good thing, something fun we can do together and make happy memories of.

"Wonderful," the woman smiles and her eyes swing to me. She appraises me but it's friendly. I like her already for not checking him out. "Clarissa, I hear you are here to teach the big guy how to ride?"

Looking back up to Jackson, I frown. Wow, he's really pushing it here. I could ruin the moment and call him out. That doesn't feel right though. He's gone through an awful lot of trouble to do this for me and I appreciate it. How could he have known?

"You seriously don't think you are small enough to fit on a horse, do you?" I ask teasingly.

His eyebrows knit together as if he actually has to think about it. "Do you think I'm too big to ride a horse? I looked it up before setting this up."

I can't help but burst into a fit of giggles at that. He looked so serious, so sincere, but now he's grinning at me and there's this twinkle in his eye that's absolutely gorgeous, especially since I know I put it there.

Giggles drying away and composing myself, I turn back towards the woman. "Yeah, I think I'll give it a try, but I haven't ridden in about three years."

"Oh, then you're an old hand. It's just like riding a bike, once you know you never forget. I'm Bridget by the way."

The three of us shake hands and then walk over to the corral. We watch the horses trot around the ring. Each is beautiful in their own right but my eyes instantly settle on a pinto mare who keeps coming over to me. She looks like she wants me to touch her. As soon as I reach my hand to her she puts her snout right out there for me. Yep, I want to ride her, she just feels right.

There is a large black stallion in there as well and I can see him eying up Jackson. Either he knows he's about to have to carry his large butt around, or he smells Jackson. They are eying each other up.

Jackson just stares right back.

This is a male thing, and I'm surprised Jackson knows what to do. But then again, he's such an alpha male he just oozes that shit everywhere.

I've always believed you shouldn't go picking a horse. They will pick you in their own way and time. If one doesn't want you, you might as well just ride a trail horse who is used to multiple riders. Keep looking until one likes you because they have a sixth sense when it comes to who they allow to ride them.

The stallion keeps making circuits around the corral.

He's investigating Jackson, watching to see what he does. I keep quiet at this and look over to Bridget.

We're both surprised that these two are so intense. I bet she wasn't planning on us even riding the stallion, probably expected us to pick a mare or gelding and go.

From the intense look on Jackson's face, I know that isn't going to happen.

I'm just about to tell Jackson to just let it go when the black stallion stops in the middle of making another circle.

Heading straight to Jackson, the horse stands there in front of him.

Waiting.

Both breathing heavily through their noses, Jackson reaches up and scratches the horse on the neck.

"Alright, big boy, you want to go for a ride?" Jackson asks.

The horse doesn't show any reaction but Jackson smiles. He looks back to us as he asks, "You guys ready?"

Saddling our horses, we lead them out of the barn. Bridget follows on a horse of her own as we make our way out. She's going to ride with us for a bit then head back to the barn. She is just here to make sure I can ride as I said and that Jackson is comfortable.

Jackson, sitting on his horse, is looking so damn sexy... It's a picture searing into my mind, one I know I will never forget.

He is huge just like the horse. The two of them are a perfect match, like they were made for each other. The stallion is very well behaved as we start out and I can tell the horse likes Jackson. Not once does he try to fight him.

The same can be said for Jackson. He looks like a natural as we start to trot.

Smiling at me, he says, "I know what my next big purchase might be."

I shake my head. Let's see what he thinks after we're done and he's sore all over.

Holy fuck balls and horses, my thighs are fucking hurting. My hips are still aching.

Fuck, horse riding is no joke at all.

She was right when she said the longer I ride the worse it will be. Thank god I don't pitch tonight.

Thank god I don't pitch the next two nights.

Groaning, I sit up on my side of the bed. I'm sore and my legs are chapped. Fuck, that was a bad idea, but it was so damn worth it.

It's the last two games of the season and I'm off for both of them. We secured the top spot in the playoffs a week ago so now all we need to do is rest up and make sure we are ready for what's to come.

Three weeks ago we started riding horses and each time I come back for more. Clarissa is so much happier now that she is back to riding. The smile on her face is always more than worth the discomfort of the next day.

I pushed it yesterday, though. I wanted to see if we could ride all the way around the ranch. The place is huge. It took some time and we had to stop to have a small picnic but it was worth it.

I still want to own horses, they are awesome.

Clarissa thinks I'm nuts for wanting to get a ranch somewhere for the off-seasons, but I think there is some merit to the thought. Then again, she isn't aware that I'm including her in that picture I'm painting of my future. Which I completely am.

These last weeks have been great and I don't see that changing. What I don't like, though, is her not being with me when we I'm on the road.

I miss her.

I want to see her more, and it's making me think about what some of the other players do. Some guys will leave their families in the city they live in and only see them when they are in town.

But a few have their girls travel with them the entire season.

I know Clarissa wants to be around to help her grand-mother, but Helen has been quite blunt with saying she can handle things on her own.

I want Clarissa on the road with me.

There's a lot of down time as a pitcher on the road. It would be awesome for her to share both it and game days with me. I don't think she has to do the entire season with me, but even a third or half would be fucking awesome.

I throw really well when we fuck the night before, and even better if we fuck on game day. Shit, I can only imagine how well I would do if she was with me the entire time.

As for what she would do, well fuck, she's always wanted to be a writer. What better time to give it a shot?

Fuck, we could even go find new places to ride horses when we are off. I know the schedule can be grueling at times, but she could always take breaks if she needed 'em.

She's going to have to quit her job or at least take a sabbatical from it.

All of that is a huge commitment though, a seriously big one on both our parts. I have been thinking about having her move in with me since she spends more time at my place than she does at her grandmother's house, at least when I'm in town she does.

As I stand, I feel a stinging slap against my naked ass cheek and then Clarissa is giggling. "Way to go last night, Champ."

Growling, I turn to her but groan as my legs protest my standing. "Fuck. I feel like an old man."

"You should, grandpa," she says, snickering. "You are creaking and popping like one when you stand."

Shaking my head, I walk towards the bathroom. "You were right, I need to get a lot more riding experience under my belt before I go that long in a saddle again."

"It comes with time, baby, but you did very well. Groucho really seems to like you when we are out riding, though, and that will help a lot."

Groucho is the big black stallion I use every time we ride. He is a big monster of a horse, but as cuddly as a lap dog.

After that first meeting, he comes straight up to me at the corral. I think at first he was letting me know those mares were his and that I should respect it. In turn, I let him know that my girl beside me was mine and he should respect that.

Alpha shit aside, he fucking loves carrots and apples.

I hear my girl walking behind me as we head into the bathroom to get ready for the day. It was a good night last night even if I'm sore as shit. Heading to the shower, I plan on using all the steaming hot water in our tank today. I need to get these muscles loose.

Fuck, fuck, fuck.

Looking back as I step in, I see that beautiful naked body and my mind goes blank. My feet stop in the middle of the glass door entrance to my shower. Staring at those breasts, I have no idea where it comes from but I have the strongest desire to see them swell for my child.

Fuck, my cock is growing harder and harder by the second.

Watching me with a twinkle in her eye, she smiles. "See something you like?"

Nodding my head, I just blurt out, "Yeah, you pregnant."

What the fuck? Did that honestly just come out of my mouth? Shit.

"I mean..."

Her eyes go wide as she asks, "Are you nuts?"

"Somewhat."

"Not a chance, buddy. I'm on the pill and until I get married it stays that way."

"We can take care of that pretty quickly, ya know..."

Fuck, it would solve a shit ton of problems with her living somewhere else.

Groaning, she rolls her eyes and shakes her head. Walking up to me, she pokes me in my stomach. "Get in there, I'm freezing. No more silly talk."

Turning on the water, I pull her close to me, "It's not

exactly silly talk. I mean... sometime in the future we will be married. It would solve all the problems with you living with your grandmother. You could move in here and go on the road with me."

Looking up, she shakes her head to clear the water from her eyes. "Yeah, but I can't do that. Grandma needs me there."

"No, she doesn't. She even tells you she doesn't."

"She is *kidding*. There is no way I could leave her alone like that, she needs me."

"What about coming on the road with me though? I mean this has been a great two months, but next season it's long spurts at times with me on the road. We will have to do something about that."

Staring at me, she quietly says, "I know, but I don't know what to do. I can't just leave her alone like that."

"Honey, she's not a frail old lady, she's only in her early sixties! Barely old enough to retire."

I take a deep breath and lower my voice as she scowls at me in reaction. "Look, why don't you come with me next week for the playoffs? You can travel with me and see part of the country. Maybe start on writing your first novel?"

Shaking her head, she quickly turns me down. "I have a job, Jackson. I can't just up and go somewhere whenever I want. I need the money."

"For what? I will provide for you. You don't need the job, especially one in the part of town you work at. It's not the best place."

She pulls away from me. "It's not that bad of a place, for one, and I'm not some traveling whore."

"What?"

"Well? What else would I be if you are paying for everything and... and... I just sit there like a trophy wife or something? I've seen them in the wives' seats... I'm not some dumb bimbo who uses her man for money."

"I never said you would be that! I just want you with me. The job is a shit job, Clarissa. You don't need it when I can provide for us both while you are writing."

I have no clue how we got so far off track... I just wanted her to shower with me. I step towards her but she steps back.

"It's not a shit job! You don't even respect my job, how could you respect me if I relied on you as my sole provider? What about if grandma loses her pension? What would happen if she fell while I was gone?"

"Clarissa, it's not like that. Look, I just want to spend more time with you. I... I didn't mean to talk down on your job. I just worry about the part of town it's in."

"Yeah, but Jackson, not everyone can be as blessed as you on what they do for a living. Most people have to work nine to five jobs in shitty parts of town all the time, because they do what they have to do."

Pulling back from me even more, she reaches for the door handle to the glass door.

"Where are you going?"

"Home... I need to think about things."

"But we had plans for today before you go to work..."

"Well, I... that has to wait. Look, I need to work. I have a job I just can't quit because I don't want to be there."

Turning off the water, I follow her out to the bedroom, dripping water all over the floor, "Come on, don't leave."

She won't look me in the eye as she quickly gets

dressed. "I need to go home. We said some stuff and I need to think about it."

Fuck! I scream inside of my head. This was not supposed to be that kind of day.

Heading out to the living room, she grabs her keys off of the coffee table, and heads for the front door. I want to tell her to stop but what the fuck can I do? Grab her keys and say no?

She walks to her car and stands there at her door, looking at me. "I'm sorry, Jackson, I just need to think."

With that she's gone.

Fuck.

It's amazing how in movies and books they always seem to find a way for someone to stop the person from leaving.

But here in the real world she just walked out my door and left me here.

The scary part of the whole thing to me is that we didn't blow up or scream and shout. We didn't even really fight.

But she left...

Because she needs to think.

She just left.

Just like that I'm driving away from the man I love.

Like an idiot!

Crap, crap, shit! What the hell is wrong with me? What the hell is wrong with him? Crap!

The drive down his driveway and out his gate is almost like going in slow motion. I know I should be turning around, going back there and telling him how much I love him and how much I want to travel with him.

But I can't. I can't leave grandma like that. I can't leave her alone, not after grandpa passed. She needs me. She needs me there with her. Even these nights away are probably a bad thing.

And work? Calling my job a shit job? Where the hell does he get off... I mean seriously, I know it's not glamorous or anything close to what he does, but it's still a job. I still have to provide for myself. Who does he think pays for my insurance? What about gas?

The more I think of things and how they were said, the sadder I get then the madder I get.

I have this ball of anger and sadness warring inside of me. I think it might actually be hurt though.

Hurt that he would think I need to be provided for. Hurt that he wants me to leave my home to be shacked up with him. That's what it sounds like to me, being shacked up with some guy as his personal little sex toy.

I have myself so worked up in a lather of anger at Jackson for being so pigheaded that when I get home I slam the front door and stomp right into my bedroom. Grandma tries to ask me what's wrong but I just wave her off. I'm too mad.

Mad and hurt. I just can't believe he would be so thoughtless of what I have in my life. He just wants me to drop it all and change everything for him.

I hear my phone buzzing in my purse but I ignore it. Screw him. If he is going to be so stupid then so am I.

Throwing myself onto my bed, I look over at the clock and sigh. Two more hours until I get to go to my *shit* job. Yay.

I roll around in the bed and grumble. I've called this bed mine for years but it's all of a sudden completely uncomfortable. It's not nearly as comfortable as Jackson's.

Getting up, I want to hit the bed like I do Jackson's big fat head. I grab a pillow off the bed, pressing it up to my face and scream my frustration into it. I feel like some teenage girl. Dammit!

Heading out of the bedroom, I walk into the bathroom.

Finishing up the shower I tried to start with Jackson sucks. I expected to be fun with him. I love it when he soaps up my breasts and just kneads them in his big soapy wet hands.

And I wanted to spend the day together before I head into work. I didn't want to spend it fighting.

I have some guilt though. Wasn't it just a week or so ago I was thinking about how things could go with us? What the future would hold for us? I didn't even imagine he would want me to travel with him so much... how could I?

I want to be good and mad at him, but I'm sad too. And the more time passes the sadder I get. We both said things that we shouldn't have.

I said things I shouldn't have.

Now that there's distance between us, I can roll the words we said to each other around in my head and chew on them. He wants to take care of me, and he wants me to write the novel I've been dreaming of writing...

Why does it piss me off? What's so wrong with it? He hasn't lied yet, but him being able to offer me everything I've ever wanted just pissed me off so much... I don't even understand it.

Shit.

Getting out of the shower sucks. I'm cold and I don't have him here drying me off. I love that part of showering with him, it's like he has to take care of me in every little way. I love that about him. I love him.

Fuck, fuck, fuck! I'm in love with a man who just made me so mad I want to end the relationship. My one and only serious relationship. Double shit.

Grandma is sitting at the kitchen table, reading the newspaper as I sit down across from her. Absently she is stirring her sweetened coffee with one hand as she flips the page of the paper with the other.

Glancing up at me, she jerks a little as if she's startled. I've never been very good at masking my feelings, and I'm so upset right now.

"What happened, honey?" she asks.

I would try to lie to her but it's useless. She's been able to tell if I'm lying since I was a little kid.

"Jackson and I had a fight," I say slowly, fighting back tears.

Standing from her chair, she comes around to me and wraps her arms around me. Maybe if she didn't pull me into a hug, I'd be able to hold it together. But her comfort is just too much. Everything I've been holding in bursts forth and silently I start crying.

It feels good to let it out, even if it's embarrassing as hell.

"We had a small fight," I explain once I'm finally able to speak again. "A small one, no yelling or anything, but it ended with me leaving and I have no clue if we can be together again..."

"Those small ones can be so much more painful than big blowouts. They can be so devastating."

Nodding my head, I say, "Yeah, I mean we didn't even scream. It was just a few words and then I'm coming home so mad I can't even look at my phone."

"What happened?"

"He wants me to move in with him."

Her eyes brighten as she asks, "That's it?"

I frown at her. "In essence, yeah… and he said I have a shit job."

She cringes. "Was there any context surrounding that?"

"That I could write full time…"

"This sounds like you're leaving a lot out, Clarissa…"

Sighing, I look down at the table. "He wants me to quit my job and travel with him next season. He said I don't need to work, especially in *that* part of town. Then said I could write and travel with him, we wouldn't have to be apart so much. He said I could come home too, but it's…"

"What in the world is terrible about any of that?" she asks with a laugh.

I just stare at her. "I would be leaving you here alone."

She looks at me like I'm nuts. "So?"

"You would be alone, Grandma. I don't feel right about something like that, you shouldn't…"

"I shouldn't what, young lady? Take care of myself like I've been doing for the past sixty-three years?" Her smile is gone now. She's got that angry look in her eyes she used to give me when I did something when I was little to piss her off.

Raising my hands defensively, I say, "I don't mean it in a bad way, but ever since Grandpa passed away…"

"Careful there, Clarissa. I wouldn't say much more. I loved that man with everything I had in me, but he was not the caretaker of me. I was and still am a fully abled woman."

"You don't understand… I mean I wouldn't feel right if you were left alone all the time."

"I would be perfectly fine, honey. What have you

planned on your life being? Living with me until I die? Because you think that you some obligation to watch over me? I, in no way, need you to do that."

Looking down at my hands again, I sigh. "No, I just... I don't know."

"Well, you need to be getting to work," she says.

I nod in agreement and start to rise but then she shakes her head.

"You need to understand something, Clarissa. That man loves you and is offering you the opportunity of a lifetime. He wants you. No one else. *You*. Are you sure you aren't just afraid?"

She walks away, leaving me with my thoughts and everything she said. I do have to be at work soon so I have no choice but to gather up my things and leave the house. I don't even know how I'm going to work tonight with all this stuff muddling up my head.

Digging around in my purse, I have to fish my car keys out and notice my phone is blinking.

Pulling out my phone, I check it and see he's sent me three messages.

Jackson: Come back. We need to finish talking.

Jackson: I shouldn't be telling you this through a text for the first time but I love you. Come back please.

Jackson: I'm here no matter how long it takes, I will wait for you.

Fuck. What am I doing?

"**I**s it bad that I have been calling my girlfriend a butthead?" I ask the pitching coach standing beside me.

I stand still for a moment then lift my leg. Taking aim, I throw the ball hard towards the catcher.

Hearing the satisfying snap of the ball meeting leather glove, I stand back up.

The coach hands me another ball.

"Don't know. I called my wife quite a few names back in our days, though. Just never to her face. That's not smart to do, they make our food when we're home."

I focus on the catcher's fingers, they show the sign for a fastball down the middle.

Reaching back, I throw the ball as hard and fast as I can. The slapping of the ball hitting the glove this time has a different sound all together.

Fuck, that felt different. Not bad, just different.

Looking over to the coach, I remark, "Well, that was different."

Nodding his head, he yells to the guy behind the batters cage. "How fast, Henry?"

"One-hundred and two." The shout comes back.

Well, fuck me. I have hit one hundred, but never been able to break that barrier between one hundred or faster.

Looking to the coach, I say, "Guess that was good pitch."

"What the fuck? Try warning a guy you can pitch that fast and hard, Jackson," Bryce says as he pulls his hand from his glove and shakes it. He grins at me. "I gotta position my hand differently if you want to throw that fast."

Nodding my head, I look over to the pitching coach. "I know I gotta pitch tonight. Mind if I try that again a few times?"

He just stares at me before he makes a decision. "Three more pitches, if anything feels off stop right away."

I nod. He is just watching out for me so I will do exactly as he says.

The first pitch I throw is exactly at one hundred.

Shit, maybe earlier was a fluke.

The second I throw is one hundred and one.

The third is thrown right as I think of Clarissa... one hundred and three.

Holy shit.

I can just feel it now, I know when it is right.

I stop though. Coach said three and three it is. It feels fucking amazing though to throw over one hundred miles per hour.

Heading into the dugout, I'm walking into the clubhouse when the coach pulls me aside. "You know they are already billing you and Raleigh to meet up at the World Championship?"

I nod my head. I've been reading the papers just as much as anyone.

Well, that and Clarissa's grandmother has been texting me about it. She has the right of it, he's a schmuck.

I've thought about asking about Clarissa when I talk to Helen, but I know better. Whatever is going on with me and her granddaughter stays with us, not her. It's not fair to get her involved in it.

Which fucking sucks because I have no clue what to do.

We've been apart for a week now. We text a little but that's it. She won't take my calls and she won't talk to me about the fight. She keeps stalling me with *needing time to think*. Fuck!

I fucking hate that fucking phrase now. Time to think. Fuck that damnable phrase!

We blew through our competition in the first of the playoff games. We have the Colorado Mountains to finish off and then it's our final games for the Championship.

There's a very real possibility we could go up against Raleigh's team, the Cincinnati Cats.

If we go up against them it's going to be fucking madness. Something deep in my bones tells me though it's going to happen.

We are going to face them, and I'm going to be throwing at that scum sucking piece of shit.

I head into the clubhouse to sit and wait. This is the part before a game that most players don't like.

The waiting, the thinking.

It never really bothered me, I mean fuck it, what's going to happen is going to happen.

Now though? Fuck it is stressing me the fuck out. I have nothing but time to think of her.

I hate this.

Looking at my phone is almost a useless chore now. It's fucking painful to see I have no new messages from her. Before she would text me all day long, even during a game. Whatever came into her mind would pop up on my phone.

I loved it, it was like living with her right beside me.

Not now though. No, I'm a man of fucking isolation.

Getting to my locker, I hesitate for once in picking my phone out of my bag. I hesitate and then I shut the door. Fuck it, I need a shower. I need to get ready for the game. It's not like she is going to fucking message me any time soon. I have to make the fucking effort.

Hot water blasts against my skin as I think through my game plan. We are up two to one. We just need to win tonight to get into the Championship—that's it. I don't need to really do anything amazing or crazy, I just need to go do my job. I need to work.

Ten minutes until I need to be out on the field, I'm physically ready. I mean it too. Physically, I'm ready to go. Mentally, I'm fucking annoyed.

Looking at my bag, I finally pull my phone out and check it. Pushing the screen button, there's a message from Clarissa. Opening the message, it immediately pops into the instant message app.

Clarissa: I love you.

Holy hell! I stare at the phone too long as I simply cannot believe she said that. I have no clue what it fucking means, and I don't care, those words let me know we will figure something out. We have to.

"Time to go, boys. Get up and let's kick some ass!" Jim, our team manager, yells to us.

Fuck. I have no clue what to say. I need to respond but I don't know what to say.

"Jackson!" he shouts at me. "Ass off the bench, move it!"

Fuck.

Looking down at the phone, I let my heart do the typing as I start to stand.

Me: I love you. Will take a flight home tonight if I can. I'll be there as soon as possible.

Returning the phone to my bag, I jog out the door and down the hall. Time to go break the Mountain's dreams of seeing the Championship.

I stand up to my full height. My arm's a little sore but nothing to worry about. Stepping back, out of the batter's box, I take a moment to collect myself.

We are up seven to one in the top of the seventh.

I don't need to do anything but try to get on base, forcing a guy to advance from third to home.

I used to be an average hitter in high school, and in college I improved my hitting. But in the big leagues I haven't done as well. They focus on my pitching in the majors more than they do anything else. If I can't hit, the coaches aren't worried about it. My pitching more than makes up for it. If I can? It's just a bonus for them.

Stepping back in, I square my shoulders and set my feet.

Watching the pitcher as he stares me down, I decide to swing on this pitch.

Don't know why but I do. Sometimes it's just an instinct, like knowing what to throw. Granted ninety percent of the time I'm dead wrong when it comes to the hitting instinct.

He winds up and then his arm is releasing the pitch. It comes at me in a blur of speed.

My arms are already swinging around as I feel the bat connect with the ball.

The actual vibration sends little tingles up my hand as the ball flies away at an incredible speed. The ball goes high and straight, flying out towards the stands.

Dropping the bat, I run my hardest for first base. Keeping my eyes on the hitting coach, he's watching the ball and then looking at me. His smile is huge as he starts to jump up and down.

Looking up, I watch the ball sail over the wall and into the stands. It's a home run!

A fucking home run! Holy fucking shit!

I slow my run down to a jog as I round the bases. I'm staring out into the crowd and there are thousands of booing and cheering baseball fans. Some of those people look really pissed as fuck. Good. Fuck 'em if they don't love me.

I raise my hands up to double high-five my team members as I step on home plate. With that we are now up ten to one.

Looking at the camera pointing at me from the dugout, I look right into it and point, winking my eye. If she's watching right now she knows that's for her.

Descending into the dugout, I get crushed as the team crowds around me, congratulating me and smacking me on the back. Damn, that fucking felt awesome. I haven't hit a home run in two years.

Jim comes over to me after the small party ends and the next batter is up at bat. Sitting next to me, he smiles and says, "Nice job, Crass. Way to hit a ball!"

"Thanks, that was awesome!"

He frowns just slightly. "I don't want you to take this as anything bad, but I'm pulling you from the game. We need you to be fully rested for the Championship games, and I want to give the relievers some throwing time out there to get them up to par."

Nodding my head, I say, "Sounds good to me. Whatever it takes to get us in the right place."

Some pitchers are very temperamental about shit like this, but fuck it. I want to win the Championship. He thinks me coming out is good for the game, then I will do it.

For the rest of the game, I sit back and watch us blow out the Mountains, thirteen to one. We made them our bitches.

The rest of the team is back in Colorado right now, settling down from the party.

We have two days off before we play our final series against the Cats. My teammates are in a hotel, having a merry time.

Not me, though, I'm flying on a redeye back to home.

I should be there before twelve-thirty, so I don't worry too much about Clarissa being awake when I get there.

My knee keeps bouncing up and down as I try to work out what to say to her. Maybe I should just club her over the head and drag her back to my house. Chain her ass to me and never let go. That would certainly satisfy the caveman inside me.

Getting to the reserved parking, I slide into my red baby. Turning her on is almost as easy as getting turned on myself. Shit, I get turned on just hearing her motor start up.

I ease myself out of the parking lot and let her open up. The freeways aren't nearly as busy right now and it feels like I'm at Clarissa's house faster than should be possible. Well, I did hit one hundred a couple of times on the way here.

Pulling into her driveway, I shut off the car. I'm not even out of the car fully before I see her front door open up.

I barely get around the car in time to have her take a flying leap into my arms. Her legs wrap tightly around my waist as she kisses me with those soft succulent lips.

She is kissing me so hard and with so much passion that I'm nearly lost in the emotions myself. My arms are wrapped so tightly around her that I want to refuse to ever let go.

Trying to resist the love of my life is like trying to fight a fire with gasoline.

Pushing her up against her Grandmother's SUV, I pull back from her.

"I love you," my voice croaks out. "I should have said that earlier."

"Oh god, I love you Jackson, with all my heart I love you. I'm sorry I was so stupid."

Wrapping her up again, I hug her tightly. Slowly I let her slide down to where she is standing on her feet.

She looks around us sheepishly and says, "Let's go home... We need to talk and make out more in private."

Snorting my laughter, I nod my head. "Wait. Whose home?"

"Our's, I'm hoping."

Nodding my head, I steer her to the passenger side of the car. "Let's see how fast we can get there."

I don't know much when it comes to how the real world of love and relationships go. I only know what I've seen from my grandmother and grandfather when he was still alive. They loved with all their hearts, and they didn't hold things against the other. It just didn't work in the long run.

Should I have held onto being so stupid about him being wrong about my job for so long? I don't know. But he isn't holding it against me.

Well, he is holding something against me but it sure isn't that.

His thick hard cock is spearing me in the stomach as he presses me tightly against the wall.

Gathering first my left hand, then my right, he holds my hands above my head as if he is holding me captive. Just the thought of being his captive has my thighs quivering, my core clenching.

He lifts my chin up with his other hand and makes

me look him in the eye. "Clarissa, let's get something straight right now. You're mine."

Nodding my head, I stare into his eyes. He has that intense look he gets when he's pitching. "Yes."

"Mine." He leans in and kisses my lips, and he doesn't bother being gentle this time. He is punishing me for leaving him, and even through my lips ache a bit I feel aroused.

He wants me so much I can feel his cock throbbing between us.

"Always," I murmur and I mean it, no more fighting it. I'm *his*. I have been since he first laid eyes on me.

I love him and I accept it. He loves me and I accept that as well. Everything else is just background noise.

He dips his head down to my neck and I can feel his teeth lightly graze against my skin before he latches his mouth there, sucking hard at my flesh. If we were animals I would be baring my most vulnerable spot, and he is making sure I know it too.

His hand leaves my chin as it slides down to my shirt. Pushing up, under the fabric, he comes to my bra. Growling, he withdraws his hand in frustration.

He pulls away from me and drags me behind him through the house to his bedroom. He isn't taking his time either. He is actually stomping. *Stomping.* His face is full of intense tension until we're finally in front of his bed.

I would be scared of the look he is giving me right now if I wasn't so damn turned on by it.

When he finally releases my hands, my fingers go up to his face, tracing the outline of the frown on his lips. Running my nails lightly through his thick beard. He is so handsome and so masculine. He puts any statue or painting I have ever seen to shame when it comes to what a beautiful man looks like.

His breath comes out in puffs and his shoulders rise and fall with the force of his breath.

His hands come to the bottom of my tight black t-shirt, lifting it up and over my head. His bright eyes go straight to the lacy bra I put on when I knew he was coming for me. It's white and very frilly, somewhat transparent, and it pushes my breasts up high.

His rough, calloused hands come up to my bra, fingertips gently brushing against my nipples as they tighten up. He stares a long time at my breasts as his fingers trace the cups then the top of the frilly fabric. It's the first time I have ever worn something like this and his reaction is telling me I will have to do it again and again.

Looking up, into my eyes, he stares for a moment before a deep growling rumble comes from his chest. He actually just fucking growled at me. Holy shit, this is fucking hot.

I'd say something, speak something out loud, but I totally don't want to ruin the moment. There's just something extremely gratifying about knowing I've brought out the grunting caveman in him.

Besides, who needs words when he looks at me like *that*? Like he's going to fuck me so hard I'll never leave him again.

His hands drop to the waist of my skin tight jeans. I just bought them today with my bra and panties because I've planned this look down to a T. I have a lot of apologizing and groveling to do, but hopefully this outfit makes up for it a little bit. Hell, it almost seems like he already completely forgives me.

I wag my finger at him and point down to the black flats I'm wearing. I giggle as he growls again, but he kneels to remove my shoes.

As he stands back up, he presses his face against my stomach, kissing me next to my belly button. It tickles with his beard, but his breath is so hot against my stomach it also gives me goosebumps.

Standing up, his hands slide up my thighs as if he can't stop himself from touching me. I can't blame him, I'm trying so hard not to give in and say *fuck the plan.* But I can't do that.

I have a plan and I'm sticking to it.

Admittedly it might not be a very detailed plan, but I want to follow it. The plan in its entirety is simple—I want him so horny he can't restrain himself. I want him to fuck me so hard and deep that I can't walk right for a week.

I want him to fuck me so hard it causes sex induced amnesia and we can't remember the fight we had. It will be just some bad memory buried in the deep recesses of our brains.

Finally reaching for the button on my jeans, I grin at him as he unbuttons then slowly lowers my zipper. I push him back from me as I slip my thumbs into the sides of my pants. I know he can see the front of my lacy panties now that the zipper is out of the way, the little pink ribbon bow on the front peeking out.

He reaches out for my waist again and I step back, shaking my head. No, I want to do this final reveal.

Slowly I turn away from him and my hands come up

to cup my breasts. My nipples are already stiff and hard as I lightly pinch them. Turning fully around, I glance over my shoulder at him. His baby blues are riveted to the swaying motions of my ass. I know full and well he loves my ass, he loves how I shake it back and forth. He loves how full it is in his large hands.

I put my thumbs in my waistband of my pants and slowly push them down my hips, revealing the thin fabric of my thong. Peeking back at him, he is all but drooling. Good.

Once I've stepped out of my pants, I turn around and smile at him. My body is now fully on display.

When we first met I was so self-conscious about my body, worried it wouldn't be right, worried it wouldn't please him. Fuck those thoughts. Watching his face as he stares at me, I know I'm just perfect for him. Shit, just looking at his hands clenched at his sides in fists I know he is fighting hard not to leap at me.

I reach between my breasts. Hidden between my cleavage is a front clasp. I want to torture him longer but I can't. My knees are locking together and there's this throbbing ache building in my core. I need him.

Unclasping the bra, I let it fall down to the floor and my breasts drop. They feel so full and heavy, bouncing against my chest.

Smiling at him, I try to sound sultry, but my voice is cracking as I ask, "Like what you see?"

In my head that sounded so much sexier than when I said it. Thankfully he doesn't seem to notice as he nods his head.

He comes to me then wrapping his arms around my waist. Kissing me hard and deep, his hand slips down to my bare ass cheek and grabs it. Our kiss doesn't last long.

He spins me around, slamming my bare ass against his pants, the rough jean fabric scraping across my tender flesh. I can feel his throbbing cock there, it's a massive bulge pushing up against my ass.

Pulling away from me, I can barely stand the loss of contact, I want him so bad. I want him so badly I'm trembling when I hear his zipper lower. Bending me over the bed, he grabs my thong and pulls it to the side.

Oh my god, he is not even bothering to remove it.

I moan out loudly as I feel the large head of his cock rubbing between my soaking wet pussy lips. His cock feels too large to fit, pushing against my tight entrance. He keeps rubbing it against me, using my own wetness as a lubricant.

I can feel the head pop into me, spreading me. My body relaxes, stretching for him.

He slides all the way in, until he reaches the thick base of his cock and can go no further.

He moans out a long, "Fuck."

"I should probably have more patience," he huffs as he pulls out then thrusts deeply back in. "But you have no idea what you did to me with that little outfit and show."

I so do have an idea, but right now I have no desire to say anything. I just want to feel his body crashing into my own. I want to revel in this connection.

My lips open in a groan as he grabs my hair, using it as a handle and pulling back. My scalp tingles and stings but it doesn't hurt. No, it's just an extra bite of sensation.

The thrusts come faster and faster as he pounds into

me relentlessly. The heavy frame of his bed creaks and groans under the force of him. He's a machine, grunting and cursing as he pistons inside me. My only regret is that I can't actually see him as he works, all I can do is feel.

Feel the swollen crown of his cock each time it bumps into the barrier of my womb. Feel my walls clamping down on him, fisting him in a tight grip, vainly trying to hold him inside me.

As the first waves of pleasure roll through me, his thrusts slow. Hips fighting and winning through my tight grip. Grunting and growling out encouragement.

The pleasure is so intense, so out of this world, I'm mindless with it. Crying out, screaming. Shuddering, and telling him how much I love him as I rock backwards.

After that first orgasm, the pressure just seems to continue to build and build. I'm so full of him, so full of sensation, I can't contain it. I explode again, coming apart all over again and then being rebuilt into something new.

I moan his name, and pledge my eternal devotion. I'm his forever and ever.

He begins to grunt louder and instinctively I know he's holding himself back, he's trying to postpone the inevitable.

I trust my hips back hard and clench down, tightening up my stomach muscles.

"Come in me, Jackson. Make me yours," I wail as another orgasm takes hold of me.

I feel him swell inside of me and he stills, filling me up with his hot sticky warmth.

His hands release my hair and he slumps against me. I don't mind his weight at all. In fact, I love it. I love this moment where we're still unraveled and tangled together. Eventually we both catch our breath. Pulling out of me, he turns me around and gently kisses me for what seems like an eternity.

When we finally both come back down from the stars, he leads me into the bathroom to clean up. He strips himself out of his clothing then pulls down my thong. By the hand, he leads me into the shower and we just stand there together, under the hot steamy water.

No words are needed as we tend to each other's bodies. I don't know which ones we would speak even if we tried. At this moment actions are more important.

Big thick towels are wrapped around me and then he lifts me up in his arms, carrying me back to bed. As he comes down beside me and pulls me into his arms, I feel at peace. Content for once in my life. I'm finally right where I need to be—with him.

After two blissful nights with Clarissa, I pitched the second night of the series. I threw a fucking goddamn shutout! A shutout during the race for the Championship.

Of course we're up against the Cincinnati Cats. I knew it would play out like this, knew it in my bones.

I did my part, I put in the fucking effort. I made sure not to leave anything to chance.

The third night, Raymis fucked up, fucked up royally. He got stuck with a bases loaded in the first inning and then gave up a home run.

Just like that we were down four to zero.

The next fucking inning he did the same fucking thing! We were eight down. Even with Jim pulling Raymis out of the game we just couldn't get ahead.

We battled back to an eight to six score, but we just couldn't get those last three runs we needed to win.

Just like that, we were two to one in a series of five.

Then last night we couldn't even find our shoes, apparently, because we lost seven to one.

Two to two.

We win tonight or they win tonight. One way or another, the race for the Championship ends tonight.

Rolling over in the bed, I toss again.

We're home now, the final game being played in Los Angeles. We should have the home field advantage, but with the last two games we've played I have no clue if it will do us any good.

Clarissa is snoring quietly beside me.

Each time I move away from her body she instantly seeks mine out. At first I find it distracting, but then the more I do it the more I find comfort in her searching for me.

It makes me think of how even in her sleep she needs to be in constant contact. I love her, and I need to be touching her just as much as she needs it.

Rolling to my side, I pull her back into my chest, resting my hand on her hip. She is perfectly shaped for me. The swell of her hip, the dip towards her stomach, the rise up towards her ribs and shoulder. I find myself tracing that line from shoulder to hip over and over again.

In my personal life I have absolutely everything I have ever wanted and more. The only thing I would add to it would be kids—sometime soon.

But professionally I'm not satisfied.

I want to win the Championship. I want to own the ring they give to each player of the team who wins it.

I want the ring, but I have never felt so useless in my

destiny than I do right now. I'm not the starting pitcher. Gerald has the start tonight.

The most I get to do is be a reliever or closer.

The manager made sure all the pitchers knew we would be in bull pen, on call, in case he needed one of us.

Fuck! I need more control than that.

Clarissa must have awakened while I was wool gathering.

I feel her hand gently guide mine to the bottom of her shirt at her hip. Pulling the shirt up her hip, she pushes her juicy ass back against my cock. She went to bed last night wearing my t-shirt and that's it. Now, with nothing between her bare pussy and me, I feel my cock stiffening with my lust.

She releases my hand as she reaches up and behind her head to lightly stroke my cheek. "Did you sleep at all, my love?"

Sighing I say, "A little."

"Did you rest enough to…" she gives me two shoves back of her ass and I can't help but laugh.

"I'll always be able to do *that,* you sexy minx."

My thick, hard cock is now nestling between her lips. She lets go of my cheek and puts her hand down, between her thighs. Guiding me into her, she sinks her pussy all the way back onto my shaft.

My breath blasts out at the end of filling her up. She is so fucking pleasantly tight for me. It's like her body was made for me and me alone.

Our hips push back and forth as we slowly and tenderly make love. This isn't one of those hurried times, we both enjoy our time as we fuck our way into oblivion.

Sometime after I have felt her coming twice on my

thick shaft, I feel myself swelling up. I erupt deep inside of her, and as I do I pinch her nipple. Squeaking loudly, she bucks back hard against me. Each thrust I push in, she is pushing back just as hard, her breath shuddering.

Releasing her nipple, I hug her tightly to me.

"You okay?" I ask as I think about what she did when I pinched her nipple.

Her breath is still ragged as she says, "Holy cow, am I ever. That was intense."

I pull her deep into my chest and kiss her neck, "I love you."

"I love you."

There is something in the air tonight, I can feel it. Shit, the hairs on my arms are rising and I can feel the goose-bumps spreading across my skin.

The stadium is packed to capacity, even the streets around the stadium are full of people. Tonight is do or die.

Watching the game as it unfolds is equal parts terrifying and exhilarating.

Early in the first, we get a man on second and third, but are unable to get a run scored.

The second inning, Raleigh, the human pile of shit he is, knocks a ball deep into center, past the wall and far into the stands. His bitch ass swaggers around the bases as he celebrates with a booing crowd.

Just like that, we are trailing one to zero.

Third gives Gerard another chance to redeem himself, but he allows a guy to steal home with a wild throw that ends up against the backstop, behind the catcher.

My heart is sinking to my stomach as I watch Gerard squeak us out of the inning but we still have been unable to score a single run.

Halfway into the fifth Gerard walks two straight batters and Jim Morrison has had enough. He makes the signal to the umpire we are making a change.

I have been lightly warming up with my throws during the last half of the inning, but when the phone rings it's Wood who gets called into the game.

It's hard hearing another pitcher get the call but I slap him on the back and keep my mouth shut. I don't blame Jim for calling in Wood, the guy is the best middle reliever out there right now.

During the final at bat of the sixth inning, Bryce comes up to the plate. There are two guys on base for our side.

On the TV mounted to the wall in the bullpen we see Bryce smiling. He has that cocky grin he gets every once in a while.

He watches two balls and a strike go by him. Then Bryce slams his bat into the next ball, blasting it deep into the right field, past the wall and hitting the upper deck of the stands.

The crowd is going berserk.

The inning ends with the next batter, but the damage has been done to the Cats. We are finally up, three to two, and it's as if the whole team has found their second wind. New life has been breathed into our game. Our bats are connecting with the ball and our gloves are snagging impossible catches.

We don't make headway through the seventh or eighth innings, but neither do they. It's the ninth when things turn to shit.

I can see Wood has been in the game for way too long when he allows two batters to get on base—one by a walk and the other by a clean line drive.

With only one out, we are looking like shit. The phone rings even before I'm aware that Jim is making a change.

Aramis stands from his seat. Aramis is our go-to closer and has been working himself loose for the last inning. I've sat down. I'm not a closer so what need do I have to loosen up anymore?

The call comes through and then a voice calls out, "Crass, get your ass in motion."

My head was not expecting that call and it seems neither was Aramis. He turns to me with wide eyes.

Shrugging my shoulders, I say, "Old man probably has a plan."

The crowd is confused at first as I walk out the door in centerfield. It's time for the closer to come out not their starter.

I start a slow jog out to the pitcher's mound. Fuck, my heart is thundering in my chest. I have never been used as a closer but I'm not going to shirk from my duty here.

Besides, I can finally control a part of my destiny.

Looking up at the board I see who the next two batters are. A wide smile splits my face as I stop myself right in front of the team. They are all looking at me like I'm half crazy.

"So I need to strike out Rogers and Raleigh," I say to the coach.

Nodding his head, he grins right back at me. "Think you can use that new pitch of yours?"

Nodding my head, I smile. "Oh yeah."

Normally, I wouldn't use this pitch too much during a regular game. I can't guarantee my arm will be able to go an entire game throwing that fast and hard.

But right now? Fuck, I got enough in me and *more* to throw hard and fast the rest of the game.

The mound clears off as Jim heads back to the dugout.

Bryce stays back for a moment and smiles. "You ready for this?"

"Fuck yeah. You ready to wear the ring?"

Nodding his head, he pulls down his mask and walks back to the plate where he squats down.

I haven't thrown this pitch besides in practice. I wasn't sure it would be reproducible in a game situation. Now, though, I have no doubts.

Getting my arm warmed up quickly, I watch the clock on the scoreboard counting down until we resume play.

Each throw I feel the momentum of the ball getting harder and faster. I keep it below a hundred though.

No sense in spooking Rogers and Raleigh.

Rogers steps up to the plate and begins to dig in his feet. He likes to crowd the plate most of the time, daring a pitcher to throw at him.

Well, fuck him. I don't like it when hitters stand too close to my plate.

I wind up and throw the ball hard and it comes within a few inches of his stomach.

It's a ball but I think it got the message across. He

stands back about six inches and gives me a nasty look. Blowing him a kiss, I grin.

The second pitch I don't bother putting any restraint on myself as I throw hard.

I can feel the ball fly into the strike zone as it slams into Bryce's mitt.

Looking to the small sign behind the plate, I see I threw it for one-hundred and one.

Rogers is left standing there as he wonders just how fast I threw at him.

Making sure to not give my skills away just yet, I throw a sinking changeup that Rogers swings too early on, whiffing right past it. And it's strike two.

One more throw and it's strike three, he's out!

Pumping my fist, I watch the crowd stomp and scream. One more batter and we've won it all, the Championship.

Raleigh walks up to the plate. He spits out a huge spit of tobacco juice onto the ground right before he grins at me.

What a nasty prick.

I think the world pauses as we face off against each other.

The world is aware of our bad blood, and the truth has gotten out somehow about what really happened.

While he is standing there I can barely concentrate with how loud everything becomes. It is absolute bedlam here—the screaming, howling and clapping is so loud I'm surprised the people haven't busted their eardrums.

Bryce calls a time out as he stands up. We haven't even begun throwing yet and he needs to talk to me? Shit, what the fuck ?

Getting up close to me, he says to me, "Dude, this is so fucking awesome!"

I can't help but go wide-eyed at him. "Did you seriously take a time out to come say that?"

He nods his head and grins. "Dude, I bet my old ladies panties are soaked by how fucking cool this is. I got half a boner myself."

Rolling my eyes, I can't believe this guy. He gives me another grin and saunters back to the plate. He nods to the umpire.

I tilt my head to the side and start laughing.

Fuck, he probably figured I was a bit tense.

Laughing a bit harder, I shake my head. I know the world is watching and wondering what the fuck just happened. Jim is looking back and forth between us in confusion.

Getting myself under control, I stare down to the plate where Raleigh is looking aggravated. He was probably ready for this shit to start. He wants to be the big man to win the Championship, to say fuck the Stars.

I ain't going to let that shit happen.

I stand up, watching Bryce signal for my fastball right over the plate.

Nodding my head, I center myself before looking at the men on base. Fuck them. Don't matter if they try to steal, I'm striking Raleigh the fuck out.

I throw the ball hard, as hard as I have been throwing during practice.

The ball streaks right across home plate and it slaps into Bryce's glove. The crowd goes quiet for a moment while they look up at the speed.

I just threw for a hundred and three.

Raleigh has a surprised look on his face as he checks for himself. Winking at him, I get back into position.

Getting ready again I look Raleigh in the face. He is confused but more than willing to try again.

I stand up, and when Bryce calls for a fastball I shake it off. When he tilts his head, I just smile at him.

Nodding, Bryce signals for the changeup. It's a good ball to throw since it can look a lot like a fastball but is about fifteen miles per hour slower.

Standing up straight, I rock into motion as I throw the changeup. It sails right into Bryce's glove as Raleigh tries to swing again but misses the ball.

Raleigh is mad now. He pulls out of the batter's box and takes a quick moment to collect himself.

During this time, though, Bryce looks me in the eye and we are both on the same page now. He wants a fastball and so do I.

Raleigh steps back into the box.

The crowd is stomping and screaming again. The towels in the stadium are being whirled around in a circle of color. It is such a beautiful sight that I want to take a picture of this moment just so I can stay in it forever.

Focusing in again, I stand up, getting ready.

I burst forward with the ball and throw it as hard as I have ever thrown.

The ball comes out of my hand and flies right past Raleigh, hitting the glove. The board shows one hundred and five.

My arm is sore from that but it doesn't hurt to watch the umpire call the final strike of the Championship.

Throwing my hands into the air I scream out in joy,

we won and I have just struck the largest cock fuck in history out.

I get plowed into from about every single player on my team as they charge to the mound in celebration. We are the champions. We won the Championship!

I wake up to the morning light as it slowly filters its way through the bedroom window. It's beautiful outside but it can't match how bright I feel inside.

I roll over and lay myself self on top of Jackson's chest. He is so handsome here in the light of day. The sun loves him and kisses his skin. My fingers lightly trace over his features. He doesn't looks so imposing now, sleeping. He looks almost boyish with his face so relaxed.

His eyes flutter open, searching his surroundings before they lock on my face. His features instantly brighten and a slow smile spreads across his lips.

"I love you," his voice rumbles out of his chest.

"I love you, Jackson."

I keep staring at him, unable to wipe the silly grin off my face. I know I must look goofy, but right now I don't care.

"Can I ask what changed your mind?" he asks quietly.

I was wondering when he would ask that. Jackson was so tense and so busy with the Championship games, we spent most of the time leading up to it just having a lot of makeup sex.

But now that the season is over, it's time to talk. Time to make the hard decisions.

"Grandma did. She kicked me in the butt... figuratively and literally."

He raises his eyebrows at me. "Really?"

"Yeah, she wanted to make sure I understood exactly how able bodied she is. She let me know that I was a fool for fighting so hard against what I wanted and needed."

"Do you want this? Do you want *us*? We'll probably be traveling a lot next season... It will be almost impossible for you to go to college..."

"I don't know about the college part. I looked into our local one and they offer a ton of online courses. I could try my hand at writing.... so I plan on holding you to that."

Shrugging his shoulders, he smiles. "Baby, I will help you in any way you want. No matter what you want to do, I will support you. We're both in this for the long haul, right?"

I nod my head and my voice almost catches when I say, "Yes, for the long haul."

"So that means marriage, kids, a farm, horses... Lots of things... "

I take a deep breath and just hold it. It's just such a relief to hear that. To know that I didn't totally screw this up. I was just so afraid of change, of losing grandma, and of relying on someone. But Jackson has proved time and time again he won't let me down. I can trust myself to love him.

"I put my notice in yesterday," I tell him and lean down, giving him a slow, deep kiss.

I love this man so much, and I have so much to make up to him. I wish him trying to give me everything I ever wanted didn't freak me out like it did... But there's no changing it now, I just got spooked. But I plan on making it up to him, over and over again.

"It's not a real job to me," I continue, pulling away and breaking the kiss. "It's not something I want to make a career out of. So I'm going to try to my hand at writing, like you suggested. I've always dreamed of being able to give it a shot."

"What do you want to write about?" Jackson asks, his eyes soft and half-lidded. His hands are roaming all over me. Brushing across my breasts then softly trailing down to my stomach.

Smirking, I say, "I want to write a romance book."

"Really? Who are the characters?" he asks, pulling me on top of him.

Settling myself on his waist, I rock my hips a bit just to hear him groan. "Well, the male lead will be a baseball player..."

"With a really big cock?" he asks huskily and thrusts his hips up.

I can't help but laugh, and my body shakes on top of him. "Yes, a baseball pitcher with a really big cock..."

Jackson laughs with me and then he's yanking my panties to the side. "Sounds like my kind of book."

The End

Disciples Crossover

Broken Wings: Royal Bastards MC

(Featuring Jude and Simon)

Disciples

Keeping Lily (Lucifer & Lily)

Stealing Amy (Andrew & Amy)

Buying Beth (Johnathan & Beth)

Breaking Meredith (Simon & Meredith)

Taking Meghan (Gabriel & Meghan)

Trapping Sophia (James & Sophia)

The Disciples: A Dark Romance Collection

The Pounding Hearts Series

Banging Reaper (Chase & Avery)

Slamming Demon (Brett & Mandy)

Bucking Bear (Max & Grace)

Breaking Beast (Alexander and Christy)

The Pounding Hearts Bundle

Pounding Angel (Emmett & Bree)

Propositioning Love (Zoe & Bryce)

By Sean Moriarty

Gettin' Lucky

Gettin' Dirty

Star Joined Series

Craving Maul

Taming Ryock